Adventurelore

Adventure-Based Counseling
for Individuals and Groups

Jason D. Holder

Learning Publications, Inc.
Holmes Beach, Florida

ISBN 1-55691-167-X

Learning Publications, Inc.
5351 Gulf Drive
P.O. Box 1338
Holmes Beach, FL 34218-1338

Printing: 5 4 3 2 1   Year: 3 2 1 0 9

Printed in the United States of America

Contents

gressive Muscle Relaxation (PMR) • Visual Desensitization • In-Vivo • Recovery Goals • Jimmy's Water Phobia – A Case Study • Physical Activity • Spontaneous Therapy with Billy – A Case Study • Ropes Course • John's School Phobia – A Case Study

Adventure-Based Staffing – The Critical Factor • Summer Adventure Programs: *Adventurelore* Style • Rule #1 – Safety • Rule #2 – No Fighting and No Ridiculing • Rule #3 – Have Fun • Adventurelore's Maine Outpost: The Program • Day One • One Boy's Story – A Case Study • Day Two • Day Three • Day Four • Day Five • Games We Play • Adventure-Trip Discipline • Defusing a Fight • Senior Adventure Programs – Ages 13 – 18 • Jamie and the Lean-to – A Case Study • Group-Experience Processing • Good-Byes and Follow-Up

Acknowledgments

The creation of this book and the philosophy and techniques it embraces is a compilation of a magnitude of influences in my life. First, my parents for modeling excellent personal skills as parents and professional skills as counselors. Their insights, support, and interest in my work have been as essential as they have been inspirational. To my fifth grade teacher, Mr. Johnson, who recognized both a learning problem and untapped positive resources. And to the many other teachers along the way who could recognize my positive qualities, however impulsive and disruptive, and tolerate my attempts at humor for modeling a manner in which would prove to be influential in my professional life.

I am grateful to my good friends and colleagues, Dwight Webb, Ph.D., Bert Whetstone, Ph.D., and Mike Volpe, M.Ed. who have shared their professional insights and experiences to help make this book complete. I am fortunate to have had the assistance of multi-author Marcia Gilford, M.Ed., Eileen Sullivan, Ed.D., and therapist Trish Sullivan, M.Ed. who donated much of their time and efforts to the fine tuning of this book.

I owe a special thanks to Dr. Gerry Storm, a behavioral pediatrician, colleague and friend who encouraged me 14 years ago to enter the world of private practice.

To my staff, especially Chris, Shawn and Karen, who collectively have contributed over forty years of expertise to the development and fine tuning of Adventurelore programs. And to the dozens of additional Adventurelore staff who possess sensitivity, intuitiveness, patience and energy who have served with a special willingness that has touched thousands of youths in a very positive and powerful way.

A special note of thanks to my editor Shirley Foor, production manager, Vicki DiOrazio, and Ram Printing for their insights and professional guidance.

To the parents and youths who have trusted themselves and their children to the Adventurelore program.

My own childhood, which is reaching the fifth decade, has been shared with two brothers, Rick and Jon, and a sister, B.J. They have helped me to maintain a special value of family and fun. B.J., a special education coordinator for a local high school has been a valuable resource in maintaining an understanding of the various resources, realities, constraints, and capabilities of the school. I have truly been blessed by the variety and degree of support offered to me by family, friends and colleagues.

And, it is to my children, Jay, Ryan, and Suzanna, who have allowed and encouraged me to let the child in me out every day. They have served as my real life training ground. Annie, my loving wife and wonderful mother of our children, has been my partner, best friend, and support for the past 22 years, and the person to whom I dedicate this book.

Individual adventure-based counseling credits its origin to the Adventurelore staff and others who possess an affinity for the outdoors and a strength in relating to youth. The concept of the adventure-based counseling experience began with Outward Bound in the early fifties. Adventure-based counseling was coined and developed by Jim Schoel and Paul Radcliffe (long-term Project Adventure staff members) in 1972. Group adventure-based programs, such as Outward Bound, Project Adventure, and the University of New Hampshire Outdoor Education Program, led by Dr. Michael Gass, have been helpful in the further development of the Adventurelore concept.

"Adventure-based counseling (ABC) takes the best of what is known in the psychology of human behavior and makes the principles come alive. Trust does not remain just a word with an abstract definition; it becomes experience with personal meaning grounded in tested reality."

Dwight Webb

"To experience difficult challenges and to persevere beyond our self-perceived capabilities is our greatest preparation for life ahead."

Jason Holder

Introduction

Adventurelore is both a place and a program of counseling for children and adolescents that incorporates the freedom of the out-of-doors with the activities that open doors to the mind and to emotions. The adventure-based program challenges the child or the adolescent to experience trust, self-confidence, and self-esteem in an environment that invites success through individual and group activities.

Adventurelore, takes counseling outside the four walls of the counselor's office, the traditional setting in which young clients generally experience difficulty with trust and open communication because they feel threatened. When the therapist waits patiently, silently for a response inside an office, often behind the barrier of a desk, it is not easy to gain the positive connection that is necessary for a healthy therapeutic relationship. We believe that traditional treatment techniques and settings are often inappropriate for the needs of children and adolescents. The adventure-based counseling activities provide " . . . a nonthreatening, noncompetitive vehicle for change. Adolescent populations are ideal for this type of experience since self-esteem in such individuals is malleable, sometimes volatile" (Kolb 1988). Surroundings do make a difference. The initial meeting of our clients is critical. Because their reasons for coming to therapy are usually related to anxiety, depression, social ineptness, and other behavioral-adjustment disorders, they are already feeling apprehensive. They have been impacted negatively by the diagnostic labeling and history of failure. They arrive at our door with skeptical compliance. Our warm, friendly, and nonthreatening greeting sets a new tone for safety with the absence of judgment.

Children who suffer from low self-esteem and low self-confidence are less likely to be honest and open in the traditional therapeutic environment. Young people, especially those with a diminished self-concept, are less likely to explore and to share their feelings when they are intimidated by their surroundings. They feel vulnerable, which further erodes their self-esteem. The adventure-based counseling program, by design, immediately helps to make the participants feel comfortable and at ease. As (Webb 1996) has pointed out " . . . adventure-based counseling takes the best of what is known in the psychology of human behavior and makes the principles come alive. The natural environment brings excitement, challenges emotions and draws a more positive sense of self to the forefront. For the participants, the experience is real, it is powerful, and it is lasting. Perhaps the best assessment of the program's effectiveness comes from a client, "I like that we can do things *and* talk about stuff. It's awful to be in a room with nothing but four walls and someone waiting for me to talk."

The Adventurelore counseling program, which was established in 1982, can be replicated. The physical setting is best with space, comfort, universality, privacy, and places to explore one's abilities. The Adventurelore Center, nestled in a forest in Danville, New Hampshire, has a sweeping view of Long Pond. The grounds include two high-ropes courses, a low-challenges course, two climbing walls, canoes, kayaks, a basketball court, and hiking and biking trails. The administration building consists of four offices, with views of the forest and lake, worn but comfortable furniture, a rustic waiting room with adventure pictures, a safety-tip dart board, and a recreation room with wall-to-wall wrestling mats on the floor.

Our counseling program, which is laid out in this book, places special emphasis on enhancing the self-esteem, the self-confidence, and the social skills of the individual. Adventurelore is designed to enhance the psychological growth of both children and adolescents who have a history of social, emotional, behavioral, or academic difficulties. Our program integrates the adventures into the individual therapy, a process that has proved to be extremely powerful.

The norm for us has been to watch the unsuccessful child begin to experience small successes that lead to still others, until communication becomes more open and effective. This is in contrast to our office-bound experiences in which the troubled youth often remained defiant and angry, literally drowning in their frustration and their inability to communicate or to believe that they were being heard. The adventure-based counseling program allows the therapist to establish a strong relationship with the young client early in the process, which allows a smoother transition into any traditional approaches that might be needed.

Adventurelore's activity-centered approach, which is designed to increase the person's experiential processing, also fosters desirable behaviors and learning. Although our therapy programs are eclectic, the activities are most often complemented by a cognitive therapeutic approach. Adventurelore not only provides individual and group therapy to children and adolescents and their families, we also provide ongoing consultation with schools.

This book is based upon more than 20 years of my experience in counseling youth in adventure-based settings, including Adventurelore. My intent is to share with counselors, graduate students, educators, and adventure programmers the experiences and the successes of the program.

It should be noted that counselors from a variety of settings can implement the ideas in many of the formats that we outlined here. It is the quality of the person in the counselor, his ability to create therapeutic connections with his clients, and not the array of equipment and physical resources that makes the difference. The success of an adventure-based counseling program is due to the persons providing the service. The therapist who possesses intuition, sensitivity, high energy, patience, and perseverance has the tools with which to be successful. This book offers ideas from our experiences which we believe will help practitioners implement their own adventure-based programs.

You are invited to use any or all of the activities and formats, which are particular to Adventurelore. As you do so, please be aware of other outstanding programs, such as Outward Bound, Project Adventure, and the National Outdoor Leadership School (NOLS). Their resources also can contribute to your adventure-based repertoire for counseling troubled children and adolescents.

1
Beginning on 'Natural Turf'

First Meeting — A Case Study

The crunch of the tires on the gravel driveway alerts me to the fact that Robbie has arrived for his first visit. As I go out to greet Robbie and his mother, I can see them exchanging words. Mom is out of the car; Robbie remains in the front seat. Robbie is definitely reluctant to get out of the car. Mom greets me with a handshake, and begins to explain Robbie's reservations about going to counseling. I walk toward the car. As I approach the door, Robbie locks it and turns his head away. I welcome him and ask if he will give me 10 minutes to show him around. Robbie ignores the offer. I assure him that he is welcome to join us at any time, and Mom and I go to the office where she begins to unburden herself by relating Robbie's troubled past and present. As we talk, I ask Mom what things Robbie likes to do. She tells me that he loves animals. My immediate insight was twofold: animals offer a nonjudgmental friendship, and I should call my wife at our house next door and ask her to let out our two Labrador Retrievers. It took no time for the dogs to arrive and check out the new vehicle, nor did it take any time for Robbie to welcome the nonthreatening company. D.J. brings Robbie a stick and continuously barks until Robbie picks it up to throw. The games begin. From the office window, I see a more relaxed posture as Robbie continues to play with the dogs. I gave him a few more minutes of this anxiety-free play. At a time when I sense it is safe, I go outside and ask Robbie, in an attempt to establish some conversation, if the dogs are bothering him. He said, "No, they're just playing with me!" A breakthrough!

At this point, a reply of more than one word is significant. I approach the dogs in a loose gait and join Robbie in the game. To ex-

pand upon the opportunity, I offer to show Robbie how the dogs will dive from the rocks into the water to retrieve. Robbie is both intrigued and receptive, so we go down to the beach. After throwing the stick into the water a few times, I swing on the long rope swing that hangs over the water, an activity which Robbie can't resist. Soon, he joins in, engaging in the therapeutic process. This scenario took place in a total of about 15 minutes, from the time Robbie presented himself as a "resistant adolescent" to his joyful participation in the process. Robbie finished our session on the trampoline and was excited about the prospect of taking on the climbing wall when he returned. Robbie felt good about himself and his counseling environment.

The goal of adventure-based counseling is to immediately establish a good client/therapist relationship and to develop a sense of trust. The first meeting with the child is nonconfrontational and nonjudgmental.*

As portrayed above, the counselor and the child often do not even enter the office during the first session, choosing instead to explore the facilities outside. Right away, the child understands that this therapy involves something different. The child sees the ropes course, the mountain bikes, the trampoline, and the lake that is available for swimming, kayaking, or canoeing. The counselor carefully searches for a positive reaction to a particular interest and pursues it with the child. Sometimes the counselor establishes an effective rapport with the child just by sitting on the dock and fishing. The activity and the natural settings in which the counseling takes place helps to stimulate communication and strong personal interactions. A nonthreatening environment allows the focus to be redirected from "I'm a problem child" to a common goal that provides the opportunity for the therapist to reduce the first-session anxiety and to maintain a healthy comfort level. Kids do best on their own "natural turf." After a day of failure at school or perceived rejection at home, most kids are generally not eager to be constrained by four walls and discuss their family, school, or personal problems. Kids need to feel good, they need to vent, to communicate, and they need to feel comfortable in order to do so. This is especially true of children with Attention Deficit Hyperactivity Disorder, or a I prefer to call it, Attention Deficit Hyperactivity Advantage, i.e., the idea of turning impulsivity into creativity and turning misdirection into direction with a surge.

I want to emphasize the importance of the counselor/child relationship. A child (including the adolescent) who feels welcomed into counseling, rather than con-

---

*For the sake of brevity, generality and humanity, we shall use the words "child" or the informal "kid" in most references to the impersonal "client." For the same reasons, we shall use forms of "he" in all references to gender, understanding and acknowledging that problems beset both genders, and that children of both genders do come to counseling. Client may be used in referring to adult participants.

fronted, develops a more comfortable and trusting attitude. The generally upbeat, nonthreatening demeanors of both the counselor and the environment help to promote a desirable initial relationship. In addition, the therapy broadens its impact as the child has fun and experiences success with the counselor in an environment of challenge and adventure. When the therapist wants to employ adventure-based techniques in a more traditional counseling environment, he may opt for a walk, an up-beat dart game, or a discussion over some "hoops." The therapist can ease the atmosphere and help the child to literally take a breath of fresh air.

Adventure-based counseling offers a variety of challenges and activities. Use of canoes, mountain bikes, a ropes course, a trampoline, archery, basketball, hiking, soccer, skating, wrestling, and cross-country skiing are some common choices of activity-based therapy. The more aggressive or active child may find an aerobic or high-activity level beneficial, while the less-active child may initially do better by addressing the issues in a canoe or on a walk. Both canoeing and walking are comfortable environments with some physical displacement, as well as a relaxed, nonconfrontative out-of-the-office setting. Other children, however, may decide that the office is the safest, most comfortable counseling environment. Some children will start by shooting hoops before an office session in a subconscious attempt to reduce their stress. The physical activity enhances the subsequent, in-office therapeutic dialogue.

Prior to the first meeting, the counselor typically has some idea of the child's history and needs. The counselor draws upon what he or she knows about this particular child, what the child has expressed an interest in, as well as his or her own intuition to determine the initial activity. The more timid, less athletic child may begin with canoeing, archery, or hiking. These activities offer a greater assurance of success and provide a good medium for nonthreatening conversation to take place. The child with a greater need to release kinetic energy may prefer mountain biking, hockey, cross-country skiing, wrestling, the trampoline, basketball, or soccer. These activities offer a greater opportunity for the child to release energies and anxieties. The ropes course, the climbing wall, and a variety of challenge initiatives offer strong confidence building and trust development. *The activity-based approach does not need to offer the wide range of activities listed above. The availability of a few options such as hiking, biking, or basketball, in conjunction with the right counseling approach, can effectively open communication, develop a comfortable relationship, displace anxiety, and enhance self-confidence.* The key, initially, is to have fun together, experience some success, and gain the optimum level of comfort in which to complete the counseling. Establishing a positive, trusting counselor-child relationship from the start is essential. The degree of verbal information gathering and true definition of the problems are secondary at this time, although very often much of that information will be conveyed naturally during the flow or intermission of activity.

The decision to include the parent or parents in the initial part of the first session is important but sometimes difficult. I have found that up until the age of 12, having a parent present can be beneficial. The child observes the parent's approval of the therapist and feels more self-assured that he will indeed come out of the session "alive." Adolescents, on the other hand, are usually ready to separate themselves from the parent. Many adolescents are in therapy because conflicts with their parents resulted in defiant behavior. Too much parental involvement can inhibit a healthy, trusting counselor-child relationship. In fact, the parent who comes to a session with an adolescent frequently dominates the conversation, and the adolescent appears tense and noncommunicative. After a short time away from the parent, in the right environment, the adolescent inevitably changes his demeanor and begins to open up. The degree to which this happens continues to amaze me.

Toward the close of the initial session, it is important that the child understand that, equally important to their activity game and challenge time, the counselor is there to help the child explore issues that are difficult for the child, and how they both can work together to think of ways to improve the child's circumstances. Although the depth and the scope of any specific problem-solving in the first session is highly dependent on the case, it is seldom too early to interject a focus on enhanced self-esteem.

2
Trust: The Foundation
for Therapy

Developing Trust

To make the most of any therapeutic experience, the therapist must establish trust. To trust is to open the door to discuss what one feels and experiences in greater depth and without fabrication. Trust means that the child can be real with you and with himself or herself, and that your support will be there. In developing that trust, you must also explain the limit of confidentiality that is imposed when the confidentiality relates to abuse and to the child being a danger to himself or herself or to others. These factors, however, can be conveyed as a form of trust that is in the child's best interest. Too often clients will refuse to open up because they fear, from experience, another breech of confidentiality. This is a sure sign that every effort must be directed toward establishing a positive and noninvasive relationship.

Trust is addressed during the first session and reinforced more directly in the second. As (Marx 1988) stated, teens, particularly those who are needy or at risk, have little trust in parental figures, little faith in the ability of parental figures to help them, and see little value in emotional expressions.

With the introduction to any new environment, children have concerns and questions about their physical and emotional safety (Feeney 1989). The adventure-based counselor takes the time to explain that the counselor is there for the child and that, with the exceptions of those issues and situations that must by law be reported, their conversations during the activities and in the office are confidential. The explanation of confidentiality may or may not be given during the first or second session, depending upon the nature of the therapeutic environment. In either case, the counselor must realize and accept that it will take more time for children who have been violated, deserted, or abandoned, or who have experienced broken trust to develop trust again. I have found that, in most of these cases, activity-based counseling that emphasizes building a positive relationship with the child shortens the time it takes for the child to develop trust.

In individual adventure-based counseling, counselors do not wait for the ropes course or a white-water canoeing experience to develop trust. They begin when the child enters the first session, when the child or adolescent feels skeptical or belligerent. Expressions such as "What do you want from me?" or "I don't have to tell you anything!" are verbal cues that it is imperative for the counselor to break the barrier of skepticism and to establish a friendly nonjudgmental, appropriately upbeat, child-focused atmosphere. It is important to note, too, that, during initial contact with adolescents, a relatively brief connection with the parent or parents is sufficient. The adolescent needs to know that the counselor is not just another parental ally.

The use of adventure-based activities helps put the child back on a more *natural turf* and heightens the comfort level. The experienced adventure-based therapist will be able to set the climate and gently direct the child into the appropriate activity. During the initial activity, it is often helpful to engage in something that both child and therapist can do together, such as canoeing, the trampoline, shooting hoops, or biking. This allows the child to see the therapist as someone who can join into an activity and not make critical judgments. In addition, trust is further enhanced when the therapist shares similar interests, which fosters more open communications. Some children may wish to attack the ropes course. The lead in selecting an activity may come from the child or from the therapist. The experienced adventure-based counselor must be aware that although the activity may not seem challenging to the therapist, it still is a new step for the child.

The ropes course offers an excellent means to establish trust. Although the course generally is an activity that is engaged in after the first few sessions, some children will opt to take on the challenge early. For those who are more cautious and fearful of the ropes course, a very gradual and supportive approach needs to be used. The child needs to know that he is safe and will not be "pressured" to go beyond what is tolerable; however, he will be encouraged to reach new goals. During the early sessions, trust-building takes precedence over successful accomplishment of the activity. Increased trust leads to a heightened level of self-confidence in the child that may enhance the opportunity for gains in trust. A child who trusts enough to begin the ropes course needs to have that trust validated and to feel the therapist's acceptance and pride in the child's accomplishment. On many occasions, I share my trust with the children. I will teach them the basics of belaying (holding the support rope) and let them belay me up the inclined log. When they see and experience that I trust them to that degree, they often are more trusting of me. I do recommend caution and prudent judgment, however.

Modeling Trust with Bobby — A Case Study

Bobby was a 13-year-old boy, with severe learning disabilities. He needed a boost in his self-confidence. After three sessions, Bobby made it to the top of the inclined log, and he decided that he wanted to belay me. I went over the procedure for a body-belay system and practiced it with Bobby. He checked out fine and was anxious to do the real thing. I climbed to about 10 feet and jumped to show my explicit trust in Bobby. Bobby, in panic, let go of the rope and jumped back. Gravity took over and I hit the ground with force. My rolling technique was in good form, as was my disposition (a critical element), and we reviewed the belaying technique. The second time around, Bobby helped me and lowered me slowly and safely to the ground. I'm not sure who was more excited over Bobby's accomplishment, but we exchanged jubilant high five's and shared a new level of trust.

Patching Broken Confidentiality — A Case Study

This case involved a 15-year-old girl who had been sexually abused, neglected, and, in her perception, betrayed by her last two therapists who broke her confidences. During my more traditional intake role in the first session, I discussed the aspect of confidentiality with her. Her response was an immediate, "Yeah, sure! What I tell you is not going to go right back to my parents, that's what my last two shrinks said!" I immediately realized that it was time to become involved in an activity together, words were not going to repair the damage. We finished the session jumping on the trampoline, having fun, and laughing. The next session was a great cross-country ski where she fell, laughed, got up, and experienced success and fun. Conversation became more free-flowing. In fact, she borrowed a pair of cross-country skis over the next week and filled prior voids in her life with a healthy activity. By the third session, our working relationship was very open and comfortable, and she reported that some important changes had begun at home. She felt better about herself and saw hope in the future. To my surprise, by the fourth session she had stopped smoking cigarettes. Trust, healthy modeling, and successful new experiences are exceptionally powerful in the therapeutic realm, especially when carefully intertwined. (This level of trust was not likely to be reached in three more traditional sessions.)

Letting the child know that you care and are there not only each week but that you also are reachable by phone is comforting to the child. To reinforce this bond of trust, call the child periodically. When the child sees that the counselor is truly interested, it is easier for the child to trust. The use of adventure-based challenges, supported by the counselor, effectively enhance the development of trust and communication with the child.

Physical Contact

Kids need to know what appropriate physical contact is and how to integrate it into their social life. It is difficult, for instance, for the highly impulsive child to maintain appropriate space and physical interactions, whether in sports or in social settings. Through discussion, modeling play, group work, and subsequent processing, the impulsive child has an opportunity to gain insight and to review his interactions.

Initial trust can be gained by openness and appropriate touch, whether in the context of congratulations for success, in joking, through physical activity, or by being supportive. Playing fair is a significant social difficulty of many ADHD, behavior disordered, and otherwise low self-esteemed children. Making an honest call against oneself, such as traveling in basketball, or a line violation in darts, is a positive method of reinforcing another form of trust while modeling fair play. Modeling fair play and positively reinforcing the child's honesty in any game or activity are important steps in developing trust. Physical contact helps to break down the child's defenses and relaxes the physical barriers that often inhibit healthy and open communication. However, the therapist must be comfortable with the contact in order for it to be effective. Playing sports in which physical contact is natural can help to reduce any awkwardness the therapist or child might have. The therapist may know from the intake information whether the child is tactile-defensive or if the child has been sexually or physically abused, and can appropriately modify physical contact. Helping youths to understand appropriate physical contact is necessary in adventure-based therapy. Therapists who wish to avoid contact are probably best suited for a more traditional form of counseling.

The lack of trust with adults is a major inhibitor in children and, especially, adolescent counseling. The application of the proper activities in adventure-based therapy, integrated with a positive, nonconfrontative and nonthreatening initial session promotes a trusting and productive counseling relationship.

In a world with a "hands off" attitude, the need to address appropriate physical contact with our clients is great. In individual adventure-based therapy, touch may be in the form of a hand on a shoulder, playing basketball, helping someone climb over an obstacle, or in various other sports, particularly wrestling. Wrestling does wonders for breaking down both physical and communication barriers and is a healthy activity to model and discuss what's appropriate physical contact. This activity is generally introduced after the counselor has an understanding of the child's needs.

In group adventure-based therapeutic programming, the Human Knot, (see Group Activities) the Board Walk, and the Acid Swamp all help break down inhibitions and remove barriers. We also have used wrestling in groups from preschool through adolescents to build self-confidence, to reduce defensiveness and to illustrate what is appropriate and inappropriate contact. The children also learn responsibility and how to play hard without causing harm to their partners. We caution that the therapist should receive technical guidance from one knowledgeable in the sport prior to using it in therapy. Our therapists have found the learning well worth the time (see the wrestling activity on page 41).

3
Self-Esteem

The majority of psychological diagnoses in children today are at least partially related to low self-esteem. Low self-esteem, after years of taking the back seat to the more prominent diagnoses of anxiety and mood disorders, is now recognized as the primary consideration of mental well-being in youths, as well as in adults.

Self-esteem refers to one's own assessment of how capable, successful, significant, and worthy one is. For many children, the lack of self-esteem, for whatever reason, has a snowball effect in that low self-esteem leads to defensiveness, poor social cueing, increased levels of failure, and decreased self-confidence. Somewhere along the line, the child's success and recognition of that success need to be acknowledged and encouraged in order to break the negative cycle.

Islands of Healing make references to Stanley Coopersmith's and Carl Rogers' individual and supportive work on self-esteem. Coopersmith found that persons suffering from low self-esteem generally viewed themselves as inferior and incapable of handling the anxieties of every day life (Shoel, Radcliff, and Crowty 1988). A young person's self-esteem is the most critical determining factor in establishing a healthy future. Giving attention to the child's self-esteem is essential to effective therapy.

William Fitts, who developed the *Tennessee Self-Concept Scale,* states that "the person with a clear, consistent, positive, and realistic self-concept will generally behave in a healthy, confident, constructive, and effective way." (Fitts 1970). He further states that "such persons are more secure, confident, and self respecting; they have less to prove to others; are less threatened by difficult tasks, people, and situations; relate to and work with others more comfortably and effectively; and their perceptions of the world of reality are less likely to be distorted." (Fitts 1970).

As discussed in Chapter 2, the counselor's objective during the first few meetings is to establish a comfortable and trusting relationship with the child. The next step is to help the child feel better about himself. The relationship-building generally begins in the first session. For a young person to have fun, to laugh, to succeed, and to have that success reinforced by the counselor is powerful therapy. The transference of energy from the counselor to the child, while often exhilarating, is an important facet of preparing the child for an activity. Children need to have fun, to laugh, to feel joy, to beam with a burst of energy. In this setting, the child doesn't just hear that he is competent, he actually experiences his competency and success and immediately begins to feel better about himself. These initial successes give the child a sense of personal empowerment, which, in turn, positively reinforces his self-esteem. Children need to experience what success feels like. The first few sessions of adventure-based therapy can and often do pump new energy and awareness into lives that have suffered from a drought of happiness. It is important for the counselor to remember that the child has often experienced significant failures. To succeed in something and have fun being actively involved in that success is essential. For a child to share those positive experiences with his therapist opens the door to trust and communication.

The level of a child's self-esteem may be assessed through the administration of a self-esteem questionnaire, an interview, psychological tests, parent and teacher reports, or by observation. Generally, a combination of three or more of these are desirable for an thorough assessment.

Cultivating Self-Esteem through Challenge and Perseverance

Without difficulty, failure, or challenge there would be little growth. If the child has no difficulties to work out during childhood, then the child cannot develop a sense of resilience. If an adolescent does not experience conflict, then conflict-resolution skills will be undeveloped. Adventure-based groups offer not only physical challenges, but challenges that center on social dynamics. Adventure-based research by Ewert (1986) indicates that participants display more anxiety and fear related to the social realm than to the physical challenges. "In the outdoor experiential environment, a variety of social/psychological-based fears might include: fear of not fitting in with the group, holding back others from reaching their goals, and appearing foolish or inept in front of others or to one's self" (Ewert 1986). The transference of increased self-esteem gained through success in adventure challenges can help to reduce the defensiveness common in children and adults with low self-esteem.

Defensiveness often erupts when the child or the adolescent is confronted with a challenge and his or her self-esteem is in jeopardy. Under the circumstances, the child may become defensive, socially inappropriate, and weakened rather than strengthened. It is important for the counselor to perceive difficulties within the individual and to address them. If a child has difficulty in an adventure-based challenge, the counselor must help the child to process that difficulty. In the past, I have talked about my fear of heights or my poor reading skills in school. This conveys the sense that it is OK (safe) to have difficulties in life and fosters an opportunity to discuss them. The counselor can help open the door to disclosure, which will give the child insight to these difficulties. The fuller understanding of the difficulties, the validation of feelings, and the sense of trust provide an excellent foundation for effective therapy and growth.

A good time to discuss the importance of one's overall attitude in life might be after a child falls short of a goal. In some cases, the counselor may find that the child is not ready to discuss his difficulty with the particular challenge. Creating a "buffer zone," or introducing an upbeat non-threatening topic, may help to reduce any feelings of failure. Of course, sometimes the kid just needs space. In small-group situations, failure presents an opportunity for others to support the one in need. The balance of healthy confrontation, empathy, and enabling are some important considerations to talk about in the group. This practical lesson can be powerful for all participants. We, as staff, may need to help initiate the supportive action at the appropriate time. Make sure all participants receive plenty of positive feedback.

Alex — A Case Study

Alex initially approached the inclined log of our ropes course with much excitement and enthusiasm. About three feet beyond the beginning, he became nervous and wanted to come down. I gave him a specific goal to reach. "Alex! See that knot on the log in front of your left foot? I'll bet you could reach that knot and step over it." After some coaxing, Alex was able to go that much farther on the log. It didn't matter whether he made it to the top. What mattered was that he was able to surpass the level he had set for himself and to succeed in the process. "That was a great effort Alex! You hung in there and went farther than you thought you could! I'm proud of you. How does it feel to be back on the ground? That's what we like to see! Next time, if you wish, you can try to go three feet farther!" Setting a small gain for his next attempt takes the pressure off and often stimulates the response of, "Oh, I can go farther than three feet more next time!" At Adventure-lore, statements like this usually result in a bet on a frappe and subsequent success. (A frappe for non-New Englanders is ice cream, milk, and a flavored syrup.) In some activities, an adjusted time or distance may be helpful to those who need to achieve some success at that particular time.

Success improves self-confidence, which, in turn, improves self-esteem. This process reduces defensiveness, which improves social functioning, which further improves self-confidence. Success is the most essential ingredient in self-esteem, and the sincere recognition of those successes by a significant adult is a critical complement to building self-esteem. Too much failure can create the opposite effect. Constantly displaying negative behavior, especially in front of others, sets the stage for social rejection and subsequent defensiveness.

The therapist must help the child to break into a more positive and successful cycle. The therapist cannot give self-esteem to the child; the therapist can, however, create the conditions that help the child gain self-esteem by taking action. Self-esteem is created by success and the resulting self-confidence; but one must **take action** in order to experience success. As the child's level of self-esteem is increased, the child's defensiveness decreases and communication improves. The better we communicate, the better we function, and the more success we have. We must help break the cycle of failure and inertia. Taking action is the key to success and to a good self-esteem.

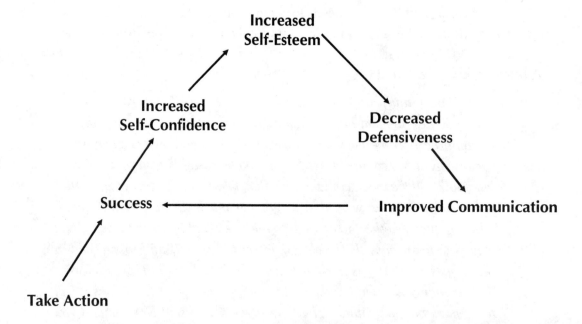

Teaching kids to pick up on social and behavioral cues from staff can substantially reduce peer ridicule for inappropriate behavior when working with at-risk kids. In a group setting, a wink of the eye or a touch on the shoulder may remind the child that he needs to take control of his behavior. A pre-rehearsed wink and tug on the ear (your own, of course) tells the child to take control or leave quietly for a nonjudgmental/unconditional time out. This reduces the negative impact among the group and allows the child to save face. The child needs to clearly understand the cues and their purpose. In groups a staff member to whom the child relates well and trusts, should present the cueing process. The message should be delivered in a positive, upbeat, non- disciplinary manner so that the child doesn't feel chastised, but knows the procedure is in his best interest. The success may come in a particular individual performance or more subtly in how the child interprets his self-worth by his achievements and/or positive interactions.

The stage for social success can be set by helping those lowest in the pecking order to succeed. The effect is greatest when that child is responsible for the group receiving a prize or achieving a privilege through his good efforts. Picking up a mess, complimenting someone, volunteering to do the dishes, answering a question correctly (this works especially well when you know the child is the only one who knows the answer), sharing with or helping someone else, or the ultimate, catching a staff member during a chase game, i.e., Capture the Flag, Wildman.

Adventure-Based Tools for Self-Esteem

The ropes course is a great tool to help develop self-confidence and self-esteem and may be used in one of the first few meetings. This modality provides an opportunity for the child, with the assistance of the counselor, to reach a goal greater than he first perceived he could achieve. The appropriate recognition of that goal achievement by the counselor fosters even greater self-confidence. The trust is strengthened by the supportive interaction between child and counselor, just as it is between the one being supported by the rope and the one holding the rope to maintain that safe support.

The fear of heights is common, and the degree of this fear is often quite significant, which provides for an even more powerful method of improving self-confidence and self-esteem. The high-ropes course helps the child overcome or reduce his fears. It's important to note that adventure-based counseling, in general, exposes children to situations "that are not only challenging but can be outright frightening" (Ewert 1989). It is essential to address the child's fears and needs as he begins to challenge himself on the ropes course. This can be done through empathy, respect, and positive recognition of his accomplishments. The child must have confidence in his counselor while the counselor is belaying him. As noted in Chapter 2, I have often allowed the child to belay me, after careful instruction and demonstration. Because there is a great deal of elaboration necessary to discuss the therapeutic effectiveness of the ropes course, we will cover it in detail in Chapter 4.

Canoeing and kayaking are non-threatening activities for most kids and offer a relatively quick sense of success — the mastery of one's own vessel with the appropriate technique gained from and recognized by the therapist. In addition to the self-esteem and the self-confidence that are gained, the opportunity for comfortable, nonthreatening early dialogue is excellent (see page 25).

The trampoline (a favorite for many) is generally an excellent source of quick success and fun for the child. Completing the basics of the bounce, the seat drop and the knee drop, reinforced by positive recognition from the therapist, bolsters the child's self-esteem. Safety is always a special concern with the trampoline so one needs to be positively careful and err on the side of caution (see page 34).

Skating and cross-country skiing have been an excellent source of success during the winter months. The key is to keep the length of activity time short enough so the child doesn't tire and become overly frustrated, yet long enough so he experiences success and fun (see pages 33 and 26).

Biking is a skill that we often assume most kids have mastered. However, for many, early failure has caused them to avoid this activity, one that is a major link to normal socialization among many youths. Resistance to such an activity must be addressed with sensitivity, patience, assurance, and a healthy degree of enthusiasm. Negotiation can often be effective to work a short biking period into the session. Helping the child to see the value of biking, as well as to experience the fun, is critical. Overcoming a fear or resistance to such a socially common activity gives a powerful boost to the youth's self-esteem and self-confidence outside of the counseling environment (see biking page 23).

The preceding activities are just some of the many tools that help to build self-esteem. Experience speaks louder than words. The critical formula for the most effective self-esteem enhancement lies within the counselor. Trust, sensitivity, intuition, and the right balance of patience and enthusiasm provides the chemistry for a successful experience. Positive recognition for the child's efforts and success builds his confidence and self-esteem. The child's recognition of his accomplishments provides greater strength to take on new challenges in adventure-based counseling, as well as in their lives.

Challenging a History of Failure — A Case Study

As Kevin came for his first session late one afternoon in February, I met him at the door. When I greeted Kevin, I saw a solemn, withdrawn 13-year-old who appeared out of any element in which he might want to be. Certainly, he did not want to be in an office where some stranger was going to cross examine him about his history of failure. It took no time to read the years of frustration firmly set in his face. After a brief hello just inside the door, which received little response, I asked what things he liked to do. Kevin responded with a low monotone, head down, "I don't know."

I offered a few suggestions, yet nothing took. I then asked if he would like to go skating, Kevin replied, helplessly, "I can't skate." I replied that I wasn't a very good skater either, but that I had skates for both of us and we could go down and watch each other fall. He semi-reluctantly obliged. Probably anything would have been better than being stuck in the office with "this stranger." I maintained a noninva-

sive conversation while we laced up our skates. Arm and arm, relying on each other for stability, we made it to the ice. Kevin was absolutely right. He couldn't skate. I wanted to support him just enough so he had a sense of skating and a sense that I would be there for him if he faltered. After about five minutes, Kevin was taking a few cautious steps by himself. He fell, and I fell. I tried to make the total crash count fairly even to help reduce any feelings of failure. "Kevin, that was your best yet! You're really getting it," I'd yell. Kevin would get back to his feet. Initially, one of a couple of awkward steps and a yell would precede his fall like the three stooges, presenting a persona of being stupid and clumsy. His history of failure was so evident. While he was down, I took a major spill and slid into him. We laughed, we had experienced a breakthrough. We rested a moment on stable ground, and then we discussed our strategy. By the 30-minute mark of the session Kevin skated from one end of the rink (about 30 yards) to the other. He truly was getting it and, equally important, he realized it. By the end of the session he skated across the pond and back about 500 to 600 yards, with just two falls. He had developed an area of competence, an island of success, and sure feet!

At the end of the session, Kevin's whole affect had changed dramatically. He spoke with enthusiasm and confidence. He needed only what we all need — to feel capable and worthy, to know that he can succeed. Kevin was in desperate need of a total program that would provide regular successes. He had no self-confidence simply because he had had no success. He had developed a very low self-esteem and found only frustration and failure in his school environment. He needed a change. With the support of his parents and of his school, Kevin was placed in a more appropriate academic environment and continued adventure-based counseling for his social/emotional difficulties. Through the coordination of school, home, and counseling, and by providing opportunities for success, and recognizing and reinforcing that success, Kevin became more successful and independent.

At *Adventurelore,* we believe that the adventure-based counselor needs to be involved in the youth's academic and home environments, as well as the therapeutic environment. This helps in both the child's transference of therapy to school or home and with the counselor's input with parents and school personnel to give the child the best possible support and reinforcement.

Much of that support comes through helping the parents to understand how to work and how to play with their child. We need to be empathetic and emphatic that parents must allow their child to try, to fail, and to succeed. We must teach parents how to encourage their children without enabling them. We need to help parents develop positive modeling strategies.

4
Individual Adventure-Based Counseling: Designing Interventions

The variety of activities that are useful in therapy is as vast as one's imagination. The implementation of the appropriate activity requires an intuitive adventure-based counselor who is tuned to the child and the context of the therapeutic process. It is common for the child to offer his additional suggestions or variations on that intervention. In sport-type activities, it is important that the children learn how to play correctly as well as fairly. Creativity is encouraged, but the therapist must reinforce the appropriate and acceptable manner of play on the playground, with peers or on teams. This is where the counselor must help connect the practice to the child's real world of school and home — this is the critical connection.

The timing and the choice of the activity are very important, and particular considerations need to be taken into account. As previously explained, a child coming in after a tense and trying day at school may benefit most from an activity that is high paced, with a low degree of difficulty. This is particularly true during the early weeks of therapy. The objective is to allow the child to vent frustration in a healthy manner, to experience fun and success, and to reach a sense of emotional well-being with which he can more objectively assess the day's highs and lows. This will further complement the more traditional forms of psychotherapy by breaking down inhibiting defenses.

Getting in Synch — A Case Study

This case in point uses a mix of more traditional therapy with adventure-based therapy. Paul, an 11-year-old boy, suffered the frustration of being a bright but severely learning-disabled child. After a stressful weekend, Paul went to school a bit tired and on edge. He experienced much of the normal frustration he experiences at school that day; however, his frustration threshold was reduced and he reacted severely to a comment made on the playground. He made cruel comments to a playmate, gestured, and swore, behavior previously uncharacteristic of Paul. Paul's denial of the circumstance was in part due to his inability to see himself in such a manner. Paul was hurt, became defensive (even offensive) and shut down. When Paul and his mom arrived at counseling that afternoon, they remained in the car for several minutes, arguing about the days events. Paul was fearful of becoming more vulnerable to the painful emotions he was already experiencing. Mike, the therapist, had established a positive relationship with Paul, and he had learned about the incident from Paul's teacher. Mike went to the car and acknowledged Paul's difficult day.

Mike: "Hey, had a tough day there, bub?"

Paul: (from underneath his jacket, hiding tear-filled eyes) "Yeah."

Mike: (turning to mom) "How about you?"

Mom: "It wasn't one of our better days."

Mike: "Well let's go inside and see if we can turn it around."

Paul: "OK." (in a soft, sad tone)

As they start inside, Mike intentionally slides a bit on the ice to help take the edge off Paul's tension. Upon entering the office, Mike changes the focus to some new pictures on the wall, pictures of kids doing a variety of adventure activities. Mike asked, "How many pictures do you see of the greatest looking guy (referring to himself, of course) in the world?" Paul responded with a "Yeah, sure." followed by, "I'm probably not up there at all." This response was a key breakthrough in Paul's previously withdrawn, yet defensive, posture. Mike needed to keep Paul positively engaged long enough to reduce the defensiveness and open the doors of communication.

Paul and Mike spent about five minutes observing and talking about the approximately 40 pictures on the board. This reduced Paul's defensiveness, and they entered the office much more ready to process the day objectively. Paul and Mike were able to work through the day's events and to understand the precedents, reactions, and consequences, as well as to discuss and to role play future directions.

After the session in the office, they went off to the woods to track some animals. Paul experienced success in his tracking and purged some residual frustrations. On the return hike out of the woods, Paul was able to see the circumstances even more clearly, which reinforced the positive direction for the upcoming days. Mike had redirected the focus from Paul's behavior to a more neutral, pleasurable subject that served to moderate Paul's emotions and to reduce his defenses. The redirection also allowed Mike and Paul to establish an open dialogue. The adventure-based activity provided Paul with success, a more positive sense of self, a fresh-air activity to recharge his emotions, and an environment to positively reinforce earlier counseling.

Many of us have experienced the defensive, sometimes resistant, child who is so emotionally constipated that the session stimulates little more than frustration and resentment. The appropriately applied activity affords the therapist the opportunity to break through the outer crust and to allow some light to shine within the child, which helps him to begin communicating more openly. Many children and adolescents resistantly enter therapy at their parents' insistence. The implications are common. "I screwed up." or "I'm the family problem." Such thoughts inhibit the initial therapeutic efforts and deserve early focus. Equally as common is the adolescent who is in conflict with authority figures, or who is in conflict with his parents because they insist that he counsel with someone he perceives is going to try to do what his parent couldn't do. For the adolescent who comes to counseling resistant and untrusting, the therapist must make counseling fun and noninvasive, or the chance for success and rapport building will likely be delayed. By beginning the therapeutic relationship on a positive note and providing for comfort and success, we reduce the level of apprehension and establish therapy as being positive. This positive opening also provides the therapist with some insight as to what activity would be most appropriate and offers the opportunity to jump right into that activity. Generally, the adolescent will volunteer which activity he would prefer, sometimes, however, the therapist needs to "make the read and take the lead" and to take it enthusiastically.

There are several things to consider when suggesting a particular activity. Generally, after the initial greeting, a brief, comfortable, noninvasive conversation will begin during a tour around the grounds. Talk about things the child likes to do, along with talk about many options for activities, takes place. Talking about the variety of activities takes the focus off the child, who is often self-conscious and nervous about his first visit, and puts it onto the fun and exciting activities. There are times, however, when the focus needs to be overtly child directed. By reviewing the information from records, intake notes, parent updates, and demeanor of your child, you will be better prepared to determine where to start and the intensity of your approach. There are some activities that lend themselves to greater opportunities to talk, for example, canoeing, whereas others, i.e., the ropes course, provide for challenge and significant success and the building of confidence and trust. The first session focuses on two very important transactions for the child: developing a comfortable, safe feeling with the therapist and experiencing some degree of joy and success, an essential factor in enhancing self-esteem.

The following is a list of activities for individual-counseling circumstances, how they are most appropriately applied, their major focus and who might benefit most.

Individual Adventure-Based Activities

The ropes course, the climbing wall, the trampoline, canoeing, and mountain biking, provide strong opportunities for success and the development of a positive, comfortable relationship. Note that for some children, however, the ropes course or a canoe may cause a heightened degree of anxiety. Therefore, the counselor will need to learn, sometimes just by asking, which activity the child would like to begin with. In choosing an activity for the session, you will want to consider the strengths, the weaknesses, and the applications of the various activities. The following list of activities will provide with a variety of adventure-based activities, their application and value as a therapeutic aid.

 Archery

☑ Major objectives: Aids impulse-control, success, fun, perseverance, safety issues

☑ Discussion opportunity: excellent

☑ Building self-confidence/self-esteem: good to excellent

Archery gives the therapist a vehicle for comfortable conversation and the opportunity to discuss safety, responsibility, and control. Some of our more impulsive kids lack the ability to pull back the bowstring, gradually focus, aim, and release. Some believe the objective is to see how quickly they can shoot all of their arrows. As the children learn to take greater control, they begin to recognize their improvement, which reinforces the lessons in impulse control. In this activity, the therapist will sometimes tell the child to stop, just before the child launches the arrow. If the child can hold his shot, he will receive an additional arrow and 15 additional seconds to shoot his arrows into the designated "man-eating" target. This level of impulse control is transferred to school and to home environments through post-activity processing.

After the child has obtained a certain level of competence, including safety, he may move to the "Imaginary Hunt." This activity is carried out in a designated wooded area where various trees are labeled as certain "man-mauling monsters," i.e., the giant man-eating Brontosaurus. The child will have four or five arrows and may have from 12 to 25 seconds to take aim and fire. The size of the tree, the distance away, and the actual number of arrows varies. Post-activity processing should concentrate on connecting his reasons for success in the activity to his possible success in school and at home, i.e., he organized his arrows, observed his time allowance, controlled impulses, focused and concentrated on his objective before firing, which improved his level of success.

Basketball

- ☑ Objective: to open communication, develop interest in a common social sport, establish positive relationship, break down barriers
- ☑ Discussion opportunity: moderate to good (the post-game verbal stimulation for some has been magical)
- ☑ Self-confidence: moderate to good
- ☑ Trust development: moderate to good

For many adolescents, males in particular, nothing seems to be a more effective opener than basketball. Basketball provides a more common ground than some of the other activities. For initial sessions, basketball provides an opportunity to open communications and to establish a relationship. Starting with hoops and engaging in a noninvasive conversation allows the therapist to gain insights and develop a safe rapport with the child. The shooting and the moving around the court allows the comfortable, physical displacement of any first-session anxiety. As the session progresses, the therapist may wish to heighten the level of stimulation by playing "horse" or "outs." A good game of one-to-one is a nice way to finish a session. It recognizes the skills and pays proper homage to the child.

The intensity of the one-to-one activity reduces anxiety and breaks down any tactile defensiveness. Basketball can be an excellent vehicle for opening communication.

Biking

- ☑ Major objectives: success, anxiety displacement, opening avenues of communication, promoting a healthy activity to be shared with friends and family, and safety skills
- ☑ Discussion opportunity: fair to moderate (good to excellent during breaks)
- ☑ Building self-confidence: variable (good to excellent)

☑ Building self-esteem: variable (moderate to excellent)

☑ Trust development: make it safe, keep it short enough to be successful (good)

☑ Provides: physical/emotional release, success (good to excellent)

Mountain biking requires multiple-speed mountain bikes with good brakes and bike helmets. It makes little sense to invest so much time, effort, and money into a child's psychological well-being without considering the safety factors. Mountain biking effectively displaces the anxiety that the child may bring into the session. It also teaches the child how to release frustration-induced tension in a positive manner. When kids feel tense, there are benefits in providing a healthy displacement.

For children who come into session more in control, I might start more traditionally in the office and finish with a 15- to 20-minute stress-inoculation ride.* Many kids, however, prefer to talk outside, ride to the woods, sometimes to a special place, to talk, and return to base. There is plenty of opportunity with mountain biking to reinforce good skills in riding, jumping, mudding, and, of course, safety.

Mike's Bike — A Case Study

Michael was referred to Adventurelore for difficulties in social interactions in school. His parents also were in the midst of a divorce. Michael received little positive reinforcement at school, from his father or from his grandparents, and he felt much less capable than his younger brother. Michael talked little with the therapists. During his first several sessions, Michael responded most to the trampoline. Although he had tried canoeing, wrestling, and a little of the ropes course, Michael really took to the trampoline. He would open up and be very candid in every session in which he used the trampoline. The therapist thought the trade-off was well worthwhile. Michael was able to discuss his limited positive experiences and the many negative ones. He also could become quite objective and insightful about certain instances in his life. Still, he lacked the self-confidence and the self-esteem to put many of his plans in motion. One of those plans was to become more physically active. It was uncommon for Michael to try something new, something that could become a regular part of his daily life and to help pull him from his home-alone, television, video game sedateness.

---

*Stress inoculation refers to preparing the body and/or mind to better handle stress (in this case, through a physical displacement of stress-related hormones through aerobic activity).

He remembered biking as a negative experience from a year ago. In a camp environment, he had tried to ride, failed, and was ridiculed by peers. To try again and risk failure was a lot to ask of Mike. We negotiated 35 minutes of trampoline and talk and five minutes on the bike. The stage was set. Michael was able to select just the "right" bike, which was the therapist's bike. The five-minute experience was preceded by a 10-minute "why I can't" delay in which he drew from a relatively large collection of excuses that were not too different from the ones he used before he would begin an arduous homework assignment. At last, Michael got on the bike with minimal assistance, rode a very short distance, and received accolades from his therapist. After two minutes of successful biking up the road and much positive attention, the therapist recommended turning back because "they were running late." Michael, on his return ride, was smiling and continually asking his therapist how he was doing. Before he reached the office, Michael realized he could ride (he experienced). He said he really liked biking and asked if we could go next time. This positive experience overcame a very inhibiting and frustrating negative experience, helped him to feel normal and capable, and helped to provide for a much needed, healthy outlet.

Canoeing

☑ Objective: open communication, promote success, introduce a positive activity

☑ Discussion opportunity: excellent

☑ Building self-confidence: good

☑ Trust development: good

Canoeing generally is a nonthreatening activity with plenty of opportunity for open communication and success. It is important to recognize, however, that many children have a real fear of drowning or of water in general. In those cases, the therapist must be very sensitive to the child's reaction and to modify the ride when necessary. Life jackets are, of course, a must.

On most occasions, I will take the stern (back of the canoe) because that is where the steering is controlled. However, there certainly are times when it is more effective to turn that control over to the child. At times, I'll have the child face backwards so that we can make eye contact. During the initial visits, however, I often find it best to have him face forward in the canoe to improve his success in canoeing, to let him focus on the surroundings, and to ensure a successful voyage. Conversation which comes naturally from this environment, is often free-flowing. When a conversation block becomes evident, the focus can be directed to the surroundings and redirected to the issues when appropriate. This technique has been most effective when the child begins to shut down. Redirecting gives the necessary break, and the skilled counselor can bring the child back to the issue. At other times, it is better to address the shut down and to attempt to work through the issue. This generally is not the case early in therapy; however, the child's success in canoeing (wet or dry) needs to be acknowledged at the end of the trip.

Canoeing Alternative — Lost in the Fog

☑ Great rainy-day outdoor activity

☑ Objective: to enhance self-confidence, to desensitize anxiety

☑ Discussion: moderate to good

☑ Building self-confidence: good to excellent

☑ Trust development: good, (contingent upon staying upright, of course)

☑ Necessities: A tarp, canoe, paddles, life jackets, and compass

The activity begins at a predesignated spot in the water in which the tarp or a blanket is draped over the canoe or the canoeist. The canoeist completes, to the best of his ability, a set course. The adventure-based counselor may be under the tarp or outside of it depending on the circumstances. I prefer to be under the tarp, which provides a great environment in which to converse. However, busy lakes and rivers may require an outside observer. Safety first. Generally, the course needs only to be three or four linked destinations. The tarp also makes this a fun and challenging rainy-day activity, and provides a comfortable outdoor office in the wild.

Cross-County Skiing

☑ Objectives: to develop self-confidence, self-esteem, healthy lifestyle patterns, perseverance, and new awareness

☑ Discussion opportunity: moderate to good.

☑ Building self-confidence: moderate to good.

Cross-country skiing is an excellent activity to get clients involved both in adventure-based therapy and their home. It provides for a healthy displacement of anxiety, encourages outside activity at a crucial time of the year, combats stress and depression (mega-aerobic), offers success, and embraces an appreciation of winter's beauty. It also is an invigorating vehicle for developing communication.

To reduce frustration, teach the necessary basic techniques of going uphill, downhill, falling, of getting up after a fall, stopping, and turning. The therapist should take a good fall or two to model perseverance. The therapist needs to recognize the client's limitations and know when to head back. Making the skiing trek a successful and fun experience heightens the likelihood of future trips and perhaps a carry-over to the home environment. We lend our cross-country ski equipment to clients who promise to use it.

Mid-winter depression, anxiety, and seasonal-affect disorder are less severe for those who get outside more during the winter months. Cross-country skiing offers a multitude of psychological, as well as physiological, benefits. The therapist must be very patient and keep in mind that the success of this session is measured by the degree of communication and the feeling of well-being the child experiences, not by the distance traveled.

Mark — A Case Study

Mark, 16, was a fairly closed and hardened adolescent who was resistant to counseling. After his mother promised him it would be different from his earlier counseling experiences, he consented. The first session entailed a comfortable greeting, a short, winter ropes-course experience, and an explanation of our counseling approach. Session two began in the office, with Mark sporting a dismal demeanor.

I started on the light side and got a clear read that it wasn't his day; he just didn't care. I told him that we were going to try something that he would think he's going to hate, but that he would actually enjoy very much. I bet him five frappes, a non-New Englander milkshake (not wanting to lose momentum), that he would enjoy a short cross-country ski. He took the bet. Thirty minutes later, after a fine ski and a surprisingly open dialogue, we came down from the last small hill out of the woods and onto the pond. The sun was just starting to set, the snow was a glistening white and the sky a bright blue. Mark stopped and paused. As he looked around he proclaimed, "God, this is beautiful!" Three minutes later, skiing across the pond, side by side in free-flowing discussion, he stopped and thanked me for bringing him out there. Mark was living in confusion and conflict at home and at school, but for this magical moment, he was free of frustration. He had displaced his anxiety and had someone to share it with in a nonthreatening environment while he enjoyed a beautiful adventure. Most significantly, he was able to express in sensitive words his appreciation for the experience. Mark's strong resistance to therapy transferred into an apprecia-

tion for the opportunity to attend therapy and to enjoy an open relationship with this therapist in a healthy wilderness environment.

Darts

☑ Objective: to promote comfort while waiting for appointments, success, nonthreatening communication, and to reduce inhibitions

☑ Discussion opportunity: good to excellent. (Note: the level of competition often reduces direct therapeutic rapport)

☑ Building self-confidence: fair to moderate.

We have a dart game in our waiting room that children use while they await their session. It helps to reduce first-session anxiety. Because darts is not always a good choice for aggression displacement, we suggest that plastic-tipped darts be used. The darts give the parent and the child an activity while they wait and fosters a comfortable, non-child focused means for the therapist to meet the child. This immediately friendly activity-centered approach reduces the degree of inhibition and anxiety often experienced by the client. Frequently, our therapists will make his or her initial contact during an impromptu dart challenge which fosters a more immediate positive relationship.

The therapist can always increase the level of success by using a flexible "official" shooting line. Darts are used quite often as a lead-in to start or to close a session. Darts provide a nonthreatening way in which to talk comfortably, to be successful, and to develop a relationship.

Exploring and/or Hiking

☑ Objective: to promote communication, success, displacement of anxiety, and to establish positive relationships

☑ Discussion opportunity: good to excellent

☑ Building self-confidence: fair to good (variable and highly counselor influenced)

Exploring engages the child in an environment in which the therapist can alter the focus of the session in accordance with the environment. For example, the session may start as a hike to explore a section of woods where there are caves. The obvious stimulation and focus is on the caves; a more subtle focus is on the child's real-life issues. This activity makes the resistant or defiant child feel less of a target of judgment in the first session. The journey to a particular destination makes conversation about specific problems less threatening. Hiking and climbing around the caves provides for a "time out" from the discussion and an opportunity for a successful experience, climbing around the rocks. The walk back brings closure to the earlier discussion and an opportunity to address particular needs and/or to reinforce a successful experience. Ideally, the journey creates an opportunity for success and comradeship while the therapist and child talk about uncomfortable issues. This activity is particularly useful with youths who need to address more immediate issues. The exploration and the destination may be adjusted so that a resting point could be used to talk through any immediate needs.

Orienteering

☑ Objective: self-confidence, self-esteem, impulse-control, organizational skills

☑ Discussion opportunity: moderate to good.

☑ Building self-confidence/self-esteem: good

☑ Trust development: good

Orienteering is generally more of a group activity, but, on occasion, it has been used in conjunction with hiking and exploring on an individual basis. It provides the therapist with an environment in which he can talk with his client, teach a new confidence/independence skill, and improve self-esteem through success. In addition, taking the time to read the compass means the child must control the impulse to run off to the desired location before a direction is carefully plotted. The transference from orienteering to "organizing one's homework prior to starting to save considerable time" or "plotting out a course of action at home before jumping in" is made clear. Kids learn so well through the experimental process. The adventure-based counselor needs to help the child transfer these skills to real life and to monitor the child's follow through. As children become proficient at finding their way through and out of the woods, they develop confidence and independence. The result could include a heightened sense of self-reliance and good decision-making. This activity is particularly good for children who feel they have little control in their lives, as well as for those who have no apparent direction. (Just maybe there is a metaphor in this one.)

Ropes Course/Climbing Wall

☑ Objective: to promote self-confidence, self-esteem, communication skills, trust

☑ Discussion opportunity: moderate to good

☑ Building self-confidence: excellent

☑ Building self-esteem: good

☑ Trust development: excellent

A ropes course is a series of rope-and-wire combinations that meander through the trees. Our courses are built among live trees. Some courses are built with telephone poles, and others are built indoors. Rope courses are constructed by running strands of 1/2" cable through bolts and trees, with ropes attached in many places. Several elements of the course use wooden platforms built into the trees for a taking-off and landing point. High-ropes courses are generally built 20 feet to 60 feet off the ground and always require a safety belay system. Low-ropes-course elements are generally one to three feet off the ground and often use personal spotters for assistance and safety.

There are a large variety of elements and combinations of elements among the different ropes courses. Each element requires different skills, and all are designed to challenge the participants. Some common elements are listed below.

The Inclined Log. A large log 25 to 35 feet long and at least eight to 10 inches thick at its thinnest end. We spirally wrap an old climbing rope around the log so we still can use the log during damp weather. The inclined log requires balance and some degree of strength. This element is often used to get up to other elements. It can be psychologically challenging by itself.

The "bear" approach to conquering the inclined log

30

The Two-Line Bridge. The Two-Line Bridge is composed of two cables running parallel and horizontally between two trees or poles. One cable is spaced about four and one-half feet above the other. This is one of the easiest elements, therefore, we like to use it early in the course.

The Giant Ladder. The Giant Ladder is another way to ascend up the course. It is a series of logs or 4 x 4 beams that are horizontally parallel to one another and connected by a cable at each end. The series of logs or beams becomes increasingly farther apart as the climber ascends, making the climb progressively more difficult. This element is generally a two-person challenge station in which the value of teamwork and communication becomes clear as the climbers continue their ascent.

The High Log. The High Log is a log running horizontally from tree to tree. The log may be long or short and generally is at least seven inches thick at its thinnest end. Some logs may be stationary whereas others are suspended from a cable, making it a more challenging "wiggle log."

The Burma Bridge. The Burma Bridge consists of a cable to walk on and two parallel rope hand rails that are connected in a "V" shape to the cable below. The rope hand rails are usually loose and add to the challenge.

The Burma Bridge

The Grape Vine. The Grape Vine consists of two parallel lines (cables), one approximately eight feet above the other. The top line has a series of ropes attached by U-bolts which hang down approximately six feet and come within about two feet of the bottom line. The objective is to walk on the bottom line while using the vertical ropes as stabilizers. The vertical ropes (grape vines) are approximately six to seven feet apart.

The Grape Vine

The Heebie Jeebie. The Heebie Jeebie consists of two parallel lines (cables), one about seven feet above the other, that have ropes or webbing crossing diagonally in the middle of the element. We find that this is one of the most difficult elements. The belayor must be very aware of the potential of the climber to tangle his belay rope in the crossing ropes. This will cause the climber to get stuck and have to go back to where he crossed the line. In essence, the climber needs to stay on one side or the other prior to crossing the junction.

The Peter Pan Trolley. The Peter Pan is a trolley system that consists of one cable, a double-pulley trolley, and two opposing wooden platforms. The object is to push off from one platform, approximately 40 feet off the ground, and be able to reach the platform at the other end, also 40 feet high. This challenge looks easy but when it comes time to make the jump, uncertainty and apprehension impose themselves. Making the jump is a metaphor for life in taking action and overcoming hurdles.

The Cargo Net. The Cargo Net is a large rope net, about 24 feet by 10 feet, suspended approximately 40 feet off the ground. Participants can climb up and down as they traverse the net to the next station.

Cargo Net

The Big W. The Big W is two parallel cables about seven feet apart. With another rope form a "W" between the top and bottom cables. As well as dealing with the fear factor, balance, coordination, and strength are all tested on the Big W.

The Trapeze Jump. The Trapeze Jump consists of a wooden platform approximately 50 feet up in the tree and a certain distance (ours is nine feet) from a trapeze bar. The trapeze bar, approximately two and one-half feet to three feet long and is suspended from the cable above. The object is to jump from the platform and catch the trapeze. Due to the stress of the jump on the belay rope, a shear reduction block system is used in the belay process. This is another element that holds a great potential for powerful breakthroughs in therapy. It is essential that the harness is re-checked to insure proper fitting.

The Tarzan Swing. The tarzan swing is a rope attached to a cable running overhead. The rope is attached to the cable about 12 feet in front of the take-off platform. The rope is approximately two feet longer than the distance from the attachment giving the sense that the person jumping will drop a couple of feet in the process; and although they do drop, the swinging action reduces the degree of sudden drop. Another great station for developing a spirit of taking action.

The Zip Line. The Zip Line consists of a platform, cable, and pulley with varying types of braking devices and back-ups toward the end. We have used both a rope-to-water zip line and dry-land zip, using the cable method. Both of our zips begin from 60 feet. The wire zip with pulley has less resistance, is faster, and, because of a lesser degree of angle, is much longer than the rope zip, which has more resistance and ends in the water. At any rate, they both have the "take action" therapeutic modality and offer a great thrill. We have come a "long way baby" when we can say therapy was as effective as it was thrilling.

A separate belay cable runs overhead of all of the elements here except perhaps the Peter Pan Trolley and the Two-Line Bridge that may use the top hand line as its belay cable.

Proper belaying techniques, equipment, and properly fitted harnesses are essential to the safety of the ropes course. In addition, the person belaying must have proper communication with the person being belayed. This section of the book is to help familiarize yourself with a variety of ropes-course elements and applications to therapy. It is not a comprehensive how-to guide on ropes courses. I recommend that before you build or run your own course you read ropes-course manuals, such as *Ropes Course Safety Manual* by Steven Webster or others, and receive proper training from persons and/or organizations who provide training programs. The ropes course is an outstanding tool to help provide a powerful therapeutic experience for one's client. Safety in operation is that tool is every bit as important as its therapeutic potential.

The ropes course is one of the most comprehensive and therapeutic tools used in adventure therapy. Because so many kids and adults have a fear of heights, the course offers an opportunity to work past some of those inhibiting and debilitating fears. The element of trust is huge in any therapeutic relationship. The therapeutic use of the ropes course fosters an opportunity to establish a strong trusting relationship in a short time. The child on the ropes course has placed his trust in the hands of the therapist, and that alone deserves recognition. Achieving and recognizing success is a powerful result of ropes-course therapy. Success should not be marked by some arbitrary distance but by the climber being able to continue beyond where he thought he could go when he first encountered fear. Recognition of that success by the therapist is important.

Encountering fear is a regular part of life, and fear can be very debilitating. Learning how to deal with fear in a healthy manner is paramount. Transferring such growth to the real world is essential if the child is to realize maximum benefit from the experience. Erickson (1978) suggests that the experience itself is powerful ther-

34

apy; yet proper transference, reinforced through a cognitive approach, seems to be the most effective means of promoting the most significant positive changes.

The climbing wall offers the additional benefits of challenge by presenting a choice of directions in which to travel, as the child attempts to overcome the obstacles. The objective is for the child to realize that in order to succeed he must use all four limbs, regardless of how much or how little each limb contributes at any given time. Most will experience a point at which they think they can climb no more, but by adjusting a hand or foot, or even by movement of the head, the climber can see the "conflict" the wall presents in a different light, make adjustments and try again. Such a experiential learning tool is very powerful and generates profound insights into real-life situations, particularly when the therapist is able to relate the experience to the child's real world.

The climbing wall is generally made of 5/8" to 3/4" exterior plywood, bolts, ropes, cable, and hand holds. Walls may be constructed indoors or outdoors between two telephone poles, or as with ours, two trees. We have found it essential for maximum safety to reinforce the attachment to the trees and frame with bolts with cable or old climbing ropes running directly through the plywood as a back-up. Strong winds can cause an outdoor wall to move some, loosening the securing bolts. The ropes or cables will keep the wall affixed to the trees. The belay cable is connected to bolt poles or trees horizontally parallel to the top of the climbing wall.

Climbing Wall

This is not in any way intended to be a challenge-wall construction guide but to give the reader an idea how the walls are constructed. Karl Rhonke and Rick Klojnsick have published *Challenge by Choice,* which gives more information about the actual construction of a climbing wall.

The wall is one of our most popular therapeutic tools in that it proposes obstacles and challenges in which the climber must persevere, make a choice in direction, and work hard to reach a particular goal.

In using the climbing wall, the ropes course, or the inclined log, the client needs to know how the belay system works. I find it helpful to allow the client to belay me first up the log assent, in order to establish a fuller understanding of how the system works, to develop greater sense of reciprocal trust,and to give a visual example of how to do it. I recommend that the counselor not go above five to six feet for two reasons. First, when the counselor goes first, the distance the counselor goes may negate any feeling of significant accomplishment by the client. Second, should the client falter as you jump, the repercussions could be concussions at the conclusion of your trip. (Did I say jump?) The satisfaction that the client gets from successfully holding you safely can be very powerful.

Four additional tips for the counselor:

1.   Use a Figure 8 arrangement instead of a body belay.

Figure 8 belay arrangement

2. With any significant weight difference, more than 20 percent, you may want to anchor the belayor to a tree or to an additional person.

3. When the person is not anchored, let him know and feel what the tug is like when and if you should fall. This will help to reduce the likelihood of a panic reaction and a subsequent noninhibited stop, drop, and roll.

4. When working with smaller children, 11 years old or younger, or whenever the belaying is a real concern and you still want them to receive the previously discussed benefits of belaying, I recommend you discretely hold onto the belayed end of the rope during your assent and descent. You enhance the safety factor, and the child still gets a sense of satisfaction and safety.

Belayor anchored to a tree

The bottom line is, don't go higher than you can safely jump, unless the child upon whom your safety depends has become fully competent. Remind children that this is something done only at counseling or with other trained adults.

Body belay, generally not recommended

Skating

☑ Objective: to develop a skill that can be used in social activities, to enhance self-confidence, to develop a healthy activity for winter

☑ Discussion opportunity: good

☑ Building self-confidence/self-esteem: good

☑ Trust development: good to excellent during the initial learning stage fair for the more advanced skater.

Skating is often an excellent choice to help get children enthused about adventure-based counseling in the winter. It provides for a healthy displacement of anxiety, encourages outside activity at a challenging time of the year, combats stress and depression, offers success, and embraces an appreciation for the beauty of winter. It also is a comfortable vehicle for developing communications.

The key to successful skating is to have properly fitted and relatively sharp skates. The therapist needs to be aware of the child's skating ability (or lack of) and be able to assist physically and verbally, wherever necessary. A fall or two by the therapist may help the challenged child feel a bit more toward the norm. For beginners, both pushing a plastic lawn chair that has arms and wearing some protective cushioning and a helmet have been helpful. Though the benefits of this activity are measured by the therapist and the child, it is best to end the activity when some success is achieved and before the feet really hurt. The degree of joy in this case is more important than the distance traveled.

Swamp Log Walk

☑ Objective: to enhance self-confidence, to challenge fears and negative perceptions, i.e., "the swamp"

☑ Discussion: moderate to good (excellent post-activity in relation to many real-life issues)

☑ Building self-confidence: good

☑ Trust development: moderate

At *Adventurelore* we made a "swamp walk" with a series of logs linked together into the swamp. There are two small floating docks at specific points on which to rest or to regain one's composure. Prior to developing this course, we would find various logs to venture out on into the swamp. This was spontaneity and creativity at their best. The challenge is to see how far one can go without a fall. Thus, each person's attempt to meet a particular challenge measures his desire to travel a certain distance at the risk of getting wet, muddy, or substantially submerged in the swamp. For many, the challenge is almost irresistible and opens great awareness in post-activity discussions on the how's and why's of choices.

Swamp Walk

♣ Tracking

☑ Objective: communication, establishing a positive relationship, setting the stage to relate real life to nature

☑ Discussion: good

☑ Building self-confidence: moderate

☑ Trust development: fair to moderate

Tracking, like hiking, provides the counselor a more comfortable, nonthreatening environment in which to develop a relationship with the child, as well as to create an appreciation for life. The objective is to identify as many tracks as one can find, to list them, and then to discuss the life styles, positive and negative, of each animal. Discussion from this would flow into having the child tell which animal he would most like to be, other than a human, of course). The conversation and the information obtained from such a session can be very insightful in directing the child on a path towards goals in his life — both long- and short-term.

○ Trampoline

☑ Objective: to provide for a quick displacement of pent-up anxiety, to gain self-confidence, and to open communication

☑ Discussion Opportunity: moderate to good

The trampoline gives the therapist an effective means to displace accumulated anxiety of the child's day and put a smile on his face. That in itself makes the trampoline an excellent tool to use to prepare the child to more effectively discuss the difficulties and the successes of his week.

When the trampoline is the main or one of only a few activity-based tools, it is very effective in displacing initial anxieties. After time on the trampoline, the session can move to a discussion area inside or outside, and then return to the trampoline for new challenges. The activity allows the child to leave therapy diffused, and with a more objective sense of how his week went. It allows the therapist to determine what techniques may be implemented to make next week better. Success and accomplishment are realized when the child completes a new trampoline challenge. Many kids are able to use the trampoline, then sit and talk immediately after jumping whereas others need a more gradual transition time, i.e., walking or canoeing.

Safety needs to be a key consideration with the trampoline. Although the newer, larger, round model appears to be a safer option than the old rectangular trampolines, safety rules, such as disallowing flips and requiring spotters at all times, are important. The trampoline is not a favorite of insurance companies, and the therapist has to carefully weigh its advantages and potential disadvantages.

Safety needs to be a key consideration

🪝 Wrestling

☑ Objectives: to promote trust, open communication, success, self-control, respect for others, and to break down barriers

☑ Discussion opportunity: moderate to good, (good to excellent - post activity).

☑ Building self-confidence/self-esteem: moderate to good

☑ Trust development: good to excellent.

We have found in both group and individual work that wrestling offers one of the greatest therapeutic benefits of all our activities. We have mats spread over the indoor activity room at our counseling office, as well as at our summer-adventure program's Maine outpost.

Wrestling helps break down physical and communication barriers, teaches kids to react less defensively when they are bumped or pushed in school or at home, and helps to develop a level of responsibility for the well-being of their wrestling partner. (It also helps to dispel the polluted view that big time wrestling on television has delivered to our youth.) Children and adolescents alike have responded well to the physical exertion and contact. Wrestling provides the opportunity for the healthy, controlled displacement of anxiety and healthy physical contact.

Wrestling Basketball. This activity is very popular with children and adolescents. It is played on wrestling mats, with a small indoor ball, and two indoor hoops at each end of the room. We generally play on our hands and knees. Safety, fun, fair play, teamwork, and respect for one another are all emphasized in this activity.

The Essence of Integrating Small-Group with Individual Therapy

Adventure-based counseling fosters an environment that is conducive to several therapeutic techniques that are often not easily employed in a more traditional setting. Children have the opportunity to observe, experience, practice, and incorporate appropriate social behaviors. Initially, an individual therapeutic relationship affords the child a one-to-one experience in which to develop a nonconfrontational, trusting relationship with the therapist. As the relationship continues, healthy modeling, cueing, stress inoculation, and improved self-esteem helps to prepare the child or adolescent for greater challenges. Small groups are often a complementary component of individual therapy. These groups range from two to four children at a time for a one- to two-hour period to a group of eight to 12 individuals on a weekend adventure program.

The integration of a cognitive behavioral approach in adventure-based counseling gives real-life insight into the way a person thinks. "Why did Eric get mad and push and swear at Sam while he was playing Moon Ball?" The therapist needs to help Eric assess whether he is happy with the outcome of such behavior, or, in some cases, to convince him that he is not. An unconditional time-out is commonly recommended before asking questions. The time-out gives Eric time to reach an emotional point at which he can think rationally. The therapist must help Eric to recognize the benefits of more appropriate play, and, after the discussion, to allow Eric to return to this activity or to a different one. The therapist must be proactive, sometimes very proactive, in shaping the activity to be a positive experience, to reinforce appropriate behavior, and to be able to process it.

Shaping the activity does not mean changing the rules to fit Eric's needs, which would reinforce his negative behavior. Positive shaping of the activity, in this case, would be to clarify rules and expectations, to be upbeat about re-entering the activity and to foster success, especially when the conflicted individuals are sharing and working together. The positive interactions during a game or activity may be rewarded subliminally or overtly. Through verbal recognition or by providing success, it is helpful when the therapist has a moderate to high degree of control of the activity's level of success. The experiences of working together and achieving success and "feeling" success and joy are powerful real-life reinforcers of positive behaviors. Post-activity processing helps to reinforce lessons on success if the process is long enough to preserve the meaning but not long enough to kill the mood.

42

In subsequent sessions, the therapist must help the child to recognize how thought before action brings about a positive outcome. This lesson will generally need to be reapplied and reinforced in small groups and in one-to-one contacts in counseling settings. Additional contact with home and school helps to establish behavioral change in the child's everyday world.

Games

Hints:

We have found it helpful for one or two staff to be players in the activity to:

1. Promote healthy modeling
2. Ensure that the ball is shared with those less likely to get it
3. Help shape the experience
4. Help heighten the level of excitement and fun through enthusiasm
5. Enjoy the fun and stay young at heart

In addition, it is helpful to have one or two staff serve as a referee and broadcaster. While they are refereeing the game, the staff also can broadcast the game by calling out names (kids love to hear their names mentioned) with exuberance, or flamboyance, if you will. These interjections, with a healthy degree of humor, takes the edge off the game and are especially effective for children with low self-esteem or for those who possess a "must win" attitude. Providing a fun and healthy game-like experience does wonders to promote healthy social attitudes.

Processing of Activities

Processing, or debriefing, is essential post-activity communication that helps to bring out the essence of the experience. A greater understanding of the behaviors involved in the action and their value, result from this process, which also fosters the positive transference of the experience to the outside world.

The processing should generally begin with a retrospective and positive insight or humorous reflection to help open the gates of communication. It is important that everyone is heard and that the freedom to appropriately express oneself is encouraged. Some questions that can help to get the comments flowing are:

-   What was the most difficult part of the challenge?
-   What helped you get through the challenge successfully?
-   What did you appreciate most that other members did or said that helped you?

- How do you feel you contributed most? (Some questions are best left open-ended.)

- What was the critical turning point of the success or the lack of success in the challenge?

- Did you (anyone) feel too inhibited to share your ideas with the group?

- Do you feel that people listened to each other?

- What would have helped the group out more?

- How does taking on this challenge relate to taking on difficult challenges at home, school, or work?

5
Reframing Stress and Anxiety

This section will focus on a generalized approach to reducing stress and helping the child to take greater control of his life.

Physical activity is probably the most effective stress-reduction tool available. This is particularly evidenced when a child comes to our office after a difficult day and needs a physical release. This is especially true with the majority of youths who manifest Attention Deficit Hyperactivity Disorder (ADHD). They have just left school, which is the most threatening and difficult environment in their lives. Imagine sitting still and having to focus on something you may not understand because you cannot appropriately process information. Many ADHD-kids have a physiological need to be active, at least periodically. Nevertheless, they are expected to be still when their need for activity increases as their frustration increases. By the time some of these kids get out of school, they are ready to explode. This condition is commonly exacerbated by academic difficulties, social difficulties, and being disciplined for un-harnessed impulsivity. The last thing these children want to do is sit in an office and discuss their problems, as generally occurs in a traditional counseling setting.

As we have said, *Adventurelore* sessions generally begin with a hearty and warm welcome and a quick read by the counselor of the type of day the child has had. There are occasions when the child may wish to talk about a particular matter first, which may be done with or without the parent. More often, they want to begin by expending some frustration-charged energy. Ideally, the activity choice should be one in which the child can discharge his/her anxiety and feel good about produces some activity-related success. Once the anxiety has dissipated and the emotions have been brought into balance, the child has a greater capacity to sort out the day's frustrations and to assess his behavior more objectively.

Aerobic activity offers direct physical and psychological benefits. Aerobic activity is well-noted for its ability to reduce the level of stress-related hormones. The benefit is, of course, best achieved when the activity is performed on a regular basis. The therapist's goal is to immediately reduce the stress and to make the activity enjoyable enough so that the child can engage in it on a more regular basis at home. Common aerobic activities that we use at *Adventurelore* are bicycling, basketball, one-to-one or two-to-two soccer, cross-country skiing, hiking, jogging (particularly in the woods), skating, trampoline, and wrestling. These activities are particularly good at reducing anxiety and restoring a more workable emotional affect. For obvious reasons, the counselor does not want to introduce a new and potentially difficult activity during periods of high anxiety. One major reason to use an aerobic activity is to restore some emotional calm and feeling of relief. We relate it to running on an i.v. of "happy juice." These kids need to displace the daily accumulation of anxiety and frustration before they reach the point at which they cannot be objective. A critical part of adventure-based therapy is providing the time to address the issues that cause the stress, and the time to implement and practice new coping strategies with the child. The emphasis here is to reduce the current level of heightened anxiety so the child can communicate. This may be a short-term goal to address an immediate crisis. For many children, this is best accomplished through: physical exertion and accomplishment (re-establishing a sense of worth); and fun (recognizing joy and the value of life). During the chosen recovery activity, the counselor needs to break down temporary barriers, pump up the client's level of self-worth, and interject the cognitive piece at the right time. These objectives are best achieved when the client's mood has changed and his defensiveness is low or reduced. The activities that work best for most (and it is very individualized) are trampoline, mountain biking, basketball, wrestling, and skating; however, others may prefer a calmer means of displacement, such as canoeing or hiking.

For children who suffer from more chronic anxiety, the objective is to help them feel better about themselves. To accomplish this, the counselor builds a very positive and trusting child-counselor relationship and carefully assesses the specific disturbance and its origin, which is commonly found somewhere in the family. Then, in a more traditional counseling format, the counselor shows the child what is expected from him and what they will do together. The child also needs a list of short-term goals that will be beneficial to his well-being in both the immediate and distant future. Because school and home are significant influences and are greatly affected by the anxiety disorder, they both should be a working part of the therapeutic plan.

For anxiety-disordered children, including those who are experiencing separation anxiety disorders, medication may also be beneficial. A referral to an appropriate child psychiatrist is recommended.

Adventure-Based Guidelines for Treating Anxiety Disorders

Adventure-based counseling uses real-life challenges that condition the child to better handle his problematic fear or fears. The use of adventure-based counseling for family sessions can be particularly useful in the treatment of anxiety disorders. Whereas anxiety disorders are commonly a family inhibitor, two or more family members can work together to better understand and overcome their fears. Family members can experience similar fears, address them, and become reciprocally supportive.

Although the anxiety-producing circumstances may be specific, an experiential-generalized approach can improve the child's ability to more clearly understand his specific disorder. For many, the success in overcoming a less-debilitating fear gives them greater confidence in addressing the major disorder. Some activities that we have found to be effective are the use of the low- and high-ropes courses, canoeing, orienteering, the swamp walk, and visiting stores and schools for agoraphobics (initially during off-peak hours). The experiential procedure should generally incorporate a systematic, desensitization approach. Some guidelines are offered by Richard Hallam (1992):

- Do not introduce a stressful circumstance until support and trust are established.
- Be clear about the objectives of the experience.
- Let the client know that you expect him to experience distress.
- Prepare the client for the experience; proactive relaxation techniques are important.
- Be realistic and prepared to make appropriate adjustments for a successful experience.
- Process the experience.

Anxiety may be caused by heredity, childhood circumstance, biological causes, and stimulus-response triggering causes, (such stressors that precipitate panic attacks). These anxieties are maintained by negative thinking and lack of addressing the environmental and treatment issues.

For many of the children who are coming to counseling for the first time, the anticipation of the therapeutic event itself can be overwhelming. Again, the need to establish a comfortable, trusting environment is essential. An adventure-based format lends itself to just that. With youths, we will most likely spend the first two sessions with the activity approach. This focus allows us to establish a very positive relationship and trust. The activity component, carefully selected, can also provide entry to the therapy ahead. Integrating the cognitive behavioral approach with adventure-based therapy establishes a strong rapport with the child which supports a collaborative working effort between the child and the counselor.

We want the client to:

- develop an understanding of his areas of concern
- develop the desire to change and to take control
- accept that he will have a caring and trusting counselor to help him
- realize that he will be capable of taking control
- learn techniques to help reduce anxiety and take control
- practice techniques of taking control
- encounter the experiential process by facing the problem in gradually incremented levels of time and intensity
- transfer the experience to other areas of his life to strengthen his self-concept and to prevent relapse

After establishing a working direction, as described above, the techniques employed are variable and dependent upon each case. Once the child has developed an understanding and has the *desire* to take control, he needs to *know* that *he* must now take action.

Dealing With Unscreened Participants — A Case Study

Pam was part of a cooperative group that was involved in a one-day team-building/communication workshop. In corporate-adult group programs in which the major focus is more on team-building, self-confidence and communication skills, advance psychological profiles are not common. The group participated in the usual challenge activities in the morning and elected to try the high-ropes course in the afternoon. The focus was on building self-confidence, individual challenges, and group support. Pam watched as a few of her co-workers went up the log and on through various elements of the course. She eventually got up the courage to try and was comforted that she could go just as far as she wanted to and could elect to come down anytime. Pam was dealing with her fear of heights and a sense of frustration. What we didn't know was that she was also in despair over final preparation for a divorce. She reached the high log, cautiously crossed it and got to her final jumping off point; the Tarzan swing. Pam froze, she could not finish the course. She hung onto the log in fear that she would lose control, a fear similar to what she was experiencing in her marriage. With coaching and encouragement from staff and peers and, eventually herself, Pam visualized herself being successful at swinging off the high log. She held the thought, jumped and swung to the ground. With a spontaneous shout of jubilance, "If I can do that, I can do anything," Pam experienced the empowerment she felt. For the first time, she felt secure in her ability to go on. Although Pam was not truly phobic, the anxiety she was encountering was taking it's toll in her daily life. Pam had felt trapped and powerless to escape her circumstance. This was a case in which the transference of gaining control/self confidence in one aspect of her life had a significant impact upon another aspect. This is a very common adventure-therapy scenario.

The degree of anxiety an adult might experience will help to determine the best method of treatment. We all experience anxiety from time to time, especially after a stress-provoking circumstance. This is normal. An anxiety disorder results when this level of anxiety is high and becomes persistent over several months.

Anxiety scales are generally rated from zero to 10, with one being the lowest level. This anxiety scale, adapted from Bourne 1996, is the scale we commonly refer to.

Level	Characteristics
0	feeling calm and relaxed
1	slight nervousness
2	becoming mildly uncomfortable, muscle tenseness, butterflies
3	noticeable physical reactions, heart rate increased
4	feeling light-headedness, uncomfortable
5-6	feeling panicky, starting to lose control
7-8	panic, moderate loss of control
9-10	feeling of terror and major loss of control

Level 4 is considered the point at which one should test oneself and hold at that point for several minutes to acclimate anxiety without feeling panic and loss of control. Others may wish to reach that point, withdraw to a lower level, recover, and return to Level 4. For others, especially initially, holding at Level 2 or Level 3 can be a major step to counter the disabling levels of anxiety. Our personal preference in adventure-based counseling is to lower the intensity to Level 3 and increase the duration of exposure to the stimulus. This provides a greater opportunity for acclimation of the stressor and a lesser degree of memorable stress. Some adults do, however, prefer to escalate the intensity. We listen to their preferences.

Relaxation Techniques

Techniques that typically complement the experiential process of adventure-based counseling in dealing with anxiety are: visualization, relaxation, systematic de-sensitization, positive self-talk, and, of course, physical activity (preferably enjoyable and aerobic in nature). A brief overview of each is offered below.

Visualization

Visualization helps the adult to see himself performing a particular challenge successfully. This may be practiced in the office, at home, or while performing a challenge activity. Professional and olympic athletes often use visualization to heighten their performance. Visualization also is used to help the challenged client to relax by imagining himself in a very special, comfortable, and/or beautiful place.

Progressive Muscle Relaxation (PMR)

PMR has less application in adventure-based counseling because the major intent is relaxation, which is generally a lengthier process. It has greater application in preparation for an upcoming stressful event to reduce muscle tension and to help induce sleep. Therefore, it can be used before undertaking a major challenge and the practical use to transferred out-of-therapy situations. PMR is performed by lying or sitting in a comfortable place and beginning with one's feet. The muscles are tightened for eight to 10 seconds and then quickly relaxed. The relaxation should be maintained for 20 seconds. Move the process to the lower legs, to the upper legs, groin and gluteus, abdominals, back, hands, arms, neck, facial muscles, and forehead. Breathing exercises and visualization can complement this relaxation process.

Visual Desensitization

During visual desensitization, we help the adult see himself in an environment or circumstance that is stressful to him. The level of visual descriptions are mild to moderate to begin with and gradually increase to higher levels on the anxiety scale. Together the counselor and the adult prepare a hierarchy of anxieties.

For example, for one who is fearful of dogs, the counselor might begin by having the adult visualize himself driving down the road and seeing a boy playing with a puppy on a lawn. Then bring the dog closer. Move from having a dog outside the office retrieving a stick to the client walking out of the office and seeing a dog 30 yards away. Then bring one close, close enough to pet. These frames are all that should be held for 20 to 40 seconds. Sometimes stories will evolve from each picture. The counselor waits to help the person visualize anxiety-provoking circumstances and then to continue seeing the picture, yet focus on relaxing. This relaxation process helps prepare the person to relax in real-life, anxiety-provoking circumstances. The counselor will have the client rate the level of anxiety (zero to 10) to monitor the stress reaction. This procedure can be used to prepare for real-life desensitization.

In-Vivo

In real-life desensitization, the client is carefully assisted to directly face the anxiety-provoking circumstance, such as with agoraphobia. Direct confrontation is the most effective means of addressing anxiety and probably the most difficult to accomplish. In more severe cases, it is recommended that you begin with visual desensitization that leads to direct confrontation. As the counselor brings the person along the path to confrontation, the increments of intensity are presented on a graduated basis, similar to visual desensitization.

Recovery Goals

As described earlier in this chapter, it is helpful for the adult to establish recovery goals. The counselor and the person need to write down the goals so that each has a copy. The person will be encouraged to reach comfort at Level 3 or Level 4 on the anxiety scale. He will have the option to withdraw from that level of hierarchy or to remain at that level until he acclimates. If he withdraws to a Level of 1 or 2 on the anxiety scale, he should relax and then re-escalate to Level 3 or Level 4 until he controls and visualizes the challenge. It is important to leave enough time in the end of the session to recover, to relax, and to process.

Although experts vary in their view of the value of promoting escape from the anxiety provoking stimuli, there is greater variation among individual clients on this matter. Some clients are able to reach a Level 4 anxiety, hold there until comfortable for a period of several minutes, whereas others will achieve success by reaching an even higher level for 10 to 20 seconds, withdrawing and returning to that level. Initially, reaching that goal and knowing they can retreat at any time is comforting and gives them the confidence that they can do it without catastrophic results. In fact, the success that results is empowering.

This movement of successive approximation toward the goal will lead to a higher level of success and allow the individual to reach a particular anxiety level and stay with it (riding it out), until the anxiety level has become the comfort level. Obtaining this sustained comfort level is necessary to transfer the experience to one's everyday living. The process is often long and enduring, and the counselor needs to show patience, encouragement, and nonjudgmental caring.

Jimmy's Water Phobia — A Case Study

Jimmy was terribly afraid of the water. His family was frustrated because it prevented them from going places in their new boat. His uncle had tried to teach Jimmy to swim by pushing him off a dock when he was four. Jimmy, now nine, would not visit friends with pools because he feared they would tease him. He feared not only the water but also, as in most phobic cases, he feared ridicule. Coming to Adventurelore on Long Pond was a major step in itself. I had a soccer ball in my hand as I greeted him at the door. Mom, in an earlier interview, had told me soccer was Jimmy's favorite sport. So soccer it was. As with most cases, Jimmy needed to establish a sense of comfort and trust in an environment that could be very threatening. We spent the better part of the session playing one-to-one soccer and joking about how good I wasn't. We later came inside and talked as we played a building-block game called "Jenga." Jimmy, although mildly reserved at first, had become comfortable. The pond out back was not an issue. Jimmy ended the session, comfortable with the environment and his counselor, and looking forward to a return visit. The next visit involved a review of last week's beating that I took playing soccer and the promise of a rematch after we explored the grounds. We looked at the mountain bikes, the climbing wall, and the ropes course, which were closer to the water. He began on the inclined log, a good starting point and the element farthest from the water's edge. His primary focus, the ropes course, had diverted some of the anxiety about the water, and Jimmy hesitantly progressed to the next element, which took him closer to the water's edge. After completing three elements, Jimmy came down from the ropes course with a sense of success and a less-threatening recognition of the waterfront. With such success on the ropes course and the relative comfort this close to the waterfront, my impulse was to invite Jimmy for a short canoe ride to the raft and back. I strained to control my eagerness. Instead, I invited Jimmy to a rematch of the soccer game. This gave Jimmy success without being overwhelmed and prevented us from engaging a higher anxiety level during the latter part of the session.

Session Two ended with Jimmy's increased trust in the counselor, greater comfort with his environment (an environment with a waterfront), and enhanced self-confidence from his success on the ropes course. Session Three began with a discussion of things Jimmy would like to do. Soccer and the ropes course were at the top of his list because he had experienced success. It was fun and comfortable for him. I agreed, and then I suggested that we might like to try new challenges as well. I acknowledged and reinforced his accomplishments of the earlier sessions. When I suggested going out to the raft in a canoe, Jimmy was quick to say that he didn't like the water. After a discussion of why Jimmy didn't like the water and how it prevented him from doing a lot of things with his family and friends, we discussed how we could "fix" that. Jimmy was willing to make a contract to work on his fear of water for 20 minutes a session and to do an activity of his choice for the next 30 minutes. Jimmy came to the next session with immediate questions on what we'd have to do and said he did not want to go on the water that day. His mother had called earlier to relay his pre-session anxiety and the fear that he'd be made to go in the water. We began the session with the review of last week's activities, his successes and the contract to work on his fear of the water. We made a list of goals that were comfortable, yet challenging, for Jimmy. Jimmy was comforted in that he did not need to enter the water just yet. Session Four, began with an exercise in which I coached Jimmy through a visualization: Jimmy, I want you to see yourself on a hot day, a really hot day. There is no breeze, and you are stranded on a desert. You are so hot. Two hundred or 300 yards away (that's three soccer fields), you can see a large pond, a shade tree, and feel a light breeze blowing the branches. You walk across the hot sand to within 20 steps of the pond and sit down. The breeze refreshes you. The coolness makes you feel more comfortable. The breeze from the water and the sound of the water make you feel better, but you are very thirsty. You need a drink of water. You go down to the pond. The water is clean enough to drink, so you cup your hands and scoop some water to your mouth. The water tastes good. Splash some water on your arms to help cool you off still more, and then return to that spot 20 steps away. You are comforted by the water and are relaxed.

This story format allows Jimmy to follow along and to imagine the water not only being safe but also comforting. We walked down to the waterfront and Jimmy put his hands into the water and splashed. We stayed at the water's edge for tow to three minutes; an amount of time that was challenging but not overwhelming. He was relieved and comforted that he could leave the waterfront without being coerced to go into the water. He received positive reinforcement for his accomplishment, which proved to be easier than he had anticipated.

Over the course of the next three weeks, we continued with these small accomplishments until Jimmy was able to get in a canoe with me and paddle around the raft and back. Gradually, Jimmy was able to transfer his ability to combat his phobia to ride in the family boat. It was very important for Mom and Dad to use great patience, as the therapist had done.

Jimmy did not attend therapy over the winter; however, the parents called with joy the next June when Jimmy was beginning to swim. They had taken up where the therapist left off, with patience, support, and encouragement. I am further convinced, each year that I practice, that child therapists, in many cases, need to place equal emphasis in working with the parents. The parents need to be better prepared to take over where the therapist has left off.

Positive self-talk complements all other forms of anxiety-reducing therapy. Positive self-talk is a matter of making supportive statements that help to promote success in overcoming the stressful obstacle. Negative self-talk, "I can't stand it," "I can't do it," gets in our way. The child needs help to recognize what he *can* do instead of what he *can't* do, what he *has* instead of what he *doesn't have,* and what he can *control* instead of "I'm *losing control."* Adventure-based therapy helps to promote self-confidence; positive self-talk helps to promote success in adventure-based challenges.

Physical Activity

If physical activity could be encapsulated and packaged, it would be the most widely prescribed drug on the market. Few would argue the fact that it would also be the most universally beneficial.

A few of the benefits of physical activity are that it:

- reduces stress
- prepares us physiologically, in a biochemical sense, to better handle future stress (stress innoculation)
- metabolizes thyroxin and adrenalin in the blood stream better. Adrenalin is released for normal preparation for the fight-or-flight syndrome. This was most helpful during the Neanderthal Era. Today's adrenalin is less likely to be used in a physiological fight-or-flight sense and is stored in the blood stream. Its accumulation increases stress levels. Physical activity reduces the buildup of adrenalin and other stress hormones
- reduces depression
- provides vigor and alertness by enhancing oxygenation of the bloodstream and oxygen levels to the brain
- enhances functioning of the cardiovascular system
- enhances body composition

Children and adolescents who are more physically capable are more likely to have a greater level of self-confidence and self-esteem. Hundreds of professional articles and books address the magical powers of physical activity. The challenge is to get young people and adults up and out and involved in physical activity on a regular basis. This can be particularly challenging for the counselor in this age of high-tech computers, televisions, and video games. It is clear that to be successful and healthy, people need to recognize the benefits of exercise, overcome inertia, and find joy in activity. The most beneficial forms of physical activity are aerobic in nature and participated in three to five times per week. If not initially enjoyable the activity becomes enjoyable in time. The adventure-based counselor has much to offer in presenting and modeling the joys of physical activity in individual, family, and group counseling.

My biggest quandary in adventure-based counseling is the situational, and sometimes accidental, use of real-life circumstances unintentionally involved with a substantial degree of success. This is part of experiential or adventure-based therapy, making the best out of an unpredicted and unplanned event. I report on a couple of real circumstances not as a recommended therapeutic procedure but on how to make the best of an accidental real-life experience.

In the adventure-based world there often are circumstances that can invoke significant anxiety without provoking retreat. In the case of Billy, a heightened anxiety was evident, although his physical state was never in peril. The ability of the counselor to make the event powerfully positive was the key.

Spontaneous Therapy with Billy — A Case Study

Mr. and Mrs. Johnson arrived with their son Billy for his first appointment in a new therapy that was acceptable to Billy. Billy was described as school phobic who didn't have any friends. The family was encouraged as they met me at the door, because Billy seemed quite responsive. As we began to talk, my two black labs came to offer their greeting as well, trotting right up to Billy before he could see them.

Not knowing that Billy was dog-and-cat phobic, I was surprised at his reaction. With a scream, Billy flew by me into the office like a bolt of lightening. His Mom was right behind him. I was initially impressed with their eagerness to begin therapy! Dad explained Mom and Billy's alarmed reaction. "So much for pets de-escalating the anxiety of therapy," I thought, as I penned the bewildered dogs, both of whom were equally ready for a session and a prescription for anti-depressants. Mom and Billy recovered in the office, as I assured them that the dogs were harmless and, more importantly, penned up. We chatted comfortably for a few minutes, and I offered to show Billy around. To my surprise, Billy allowed his parents to leave the center, as long as they promised to be back well before the session was over. Billy canoed in an area that was a safe distance from the cats and dogs and was proud of his success. He later went up to the mini-gym to shoot some baskets as we talked. Billy came back to the topic of dogs and decided that he would like to, or would be willing to, see the dogs, as long as they couldn't get near him. So Billy went to the balcony overlooking the water as I let one dog out. D.J., the therapy dog, was the chosen one because he is always willing to respond to any thrown object and return it to the thrower. Billy was able to observe D.J.'s responsiveness safely from 20 feet above. After a couple of throws I asked Billy to throw the stick for D.J. while he was safely out of reach. Billy threw the stick into the water, and D.J. appropriately brought it back under the balcony. Billy experienced the dog responding to him in a positive way. Before the session was over, Billy patted the dog. This however was preceded by Billy's Mom, also dog phobic, patting the dog. Billy needed to experience a safe relationship with the dog, and his mother (whom I now affectionately call "the dog catcher") needed to model a healthier response to stressors. Billy still experiences some anxiety with dogs and cats, but his reaction is much less reactive and more in control. Billy has increased his level of control over his school phobia and is now doing well in a private-school environment, which allowed him to gradually make the transition to the new setting and the time to see the counselor as deemed necessary. At last report, Billy was doing well in his new school environment, socially as well as academically, and is involved in a sports program. Billy has even asked his parents for a dog.

Family counseling, school consultations and programs, and adventure-based-counseling focusing on a variety of challenges both at the center and at school were and are intricate parts of his therapeutic program.

The Giant Ladder

Ropes Course

The ropes course lends itself best to anxiety disorders in that it provides a medium to overcome a very natural fear. Anxiety-disordered children have fears that control their lives. The ropes course can help them to make a conscious effort to overcome their fears. They can choose to proceed one step at a time, with positive support, to challenge and to overcome their fears. Children will generally do better after a couple of sessions of less-challenging or anxiety- provoking activities in which a good degree of trust and communication has already been established.

Once we have established the trust in the counselor and the belay system, then the child may begin his assent on the log or wall. I generally prefer the log initially, because the focus is more on the psychological than on the physical requirements of the wall. There are times, however, that redirecting one's focus to the physical challenge is beneficial.

I have found it particularly beneficial to keep the belay rope tight, especially if the child steps off the log at a lower height to test the system's security. Once the child steps off and experiences no downward vertical movement, his fears are substantially reduced. He is likely to continue the challenge and to strengthen his level of confidence.

It is important to establish a goal that the child can reach. Doing so will typically decrease the level of anxiety and frustration and foster a more necessary gradual flow of success. When the child reaches a certain level, and you feel strongly that a certain distance is obtainable, you may suggest that as a goal. This will encourage and enhance the child's satisfaction that he was challenged and succeeded. Remember, the goal needs to be right for the child, not for the therapist or the parent. Positive feedback and reassurance are critical to help fearful participants through any challenge. It is important for the child to transfer the feeling of support from challenge activities to real-life problems.

As we break from the challenge activity to the process activity, we need to talk with the child about his feelings and beliefs about his inhibiting anxiety. From the moment in which the anxiety begins to escalate to an inhibiting or debilitating state, it is important to look at the questions listed below, which will help the counselor to frame and transfer the experience.

- When did you first become frightened?
- What are you feeling now?
- What was the hardest part? Why?
- What helped you to continue?
- What positive thoughts or visualizations were most effective?
- How can you apply your challenge on the ropes course to other anxiety-provoking circumstances?

During the next meeting, the counselor should talk about the last session's successful challenge, reinforce its significance, and apply the learned anxiety-reducing techniques to the specific primary anxiety problem. Questions such as "How is your fear of going up the log like your fear of leaving home or going to school?" or "What did you do to allow yourself to get beyond that point in which initial fear may have prevented you from going any further?" or "What is your biggest fear about going to school?" (One question at a time please.) Once the counselor understands the most significant fear, then he can address it through individual sessions that involve an increased challenge load. The desensitization process, which is implemented and tested in the right adventure/activity-based therapeutic environment and transferred to the school and/or home environment, lends itself beautifully to the therapeutic process.

John's School Phobia — A Case Study

John had experienced great difficulty in physically attending school for a number of years. He had to repeat one year because of excessive absences. He had tried a variety of medications and still was unable to attend. John did not fear rejection by peers or teachers, nor did his fear seem to be related to academic work. John feared that his anxiety would cause him to "freak out," to faint, or to lose control in class.

The presence of "spinning" vertigo was ruled out. During our first session of canoeing, John talked openly about his fears. He had been out of school for two weeks and was again in danger of failing for the school year. Time being of the essence, I saw John three days in the first week and built a substantial degree of trust. John agreed to be in school by the next Monday. On day two, we used the ropes course to further develop a trusting relationship and practiced methods of relaxation through breathing and visualization. Prior to closing the session, we framed the challenging moments and related them to his fears at school. As challenging as the ropes course was, John informed me that it was no contest, his reaction to school was much more severe. We applied what we could of the ropes-course experience to the techniques used at school. Sunday was a test run for me to drive John to the school, walk up to the door, and go home.

John had succeeded and could compare that to the ropes course experience. We had decided, with school personnel, to have the guidance counselor meet with John and to provide a safe retreat for John in his office, whenever John felt he might become overwhelmed. Having a safe haven in school helped reduce his anxiety level. Arrangements were made for John to start school with one period a day and to add one period every two days, until two thirds of the day was reached. When I arrived at John's house on Monday morning, he was experiencing substantial concern about making it to school. We swung by my office and played 15 minutes of basketball. At the end of the 15 minutes much of John's anxiety was displaced, so off to school we went. John's homework, among various social challenges, includes regular physical activity and positive visualization. The reduction in John's anxiety level was greatly enhanced physically. John continues to recognize the need to physically displace his anxieties as part of his therapeutic regime.

Relaxation techniques are also effectively implemented in the adventure-based environment and are particularly helpful in treating anxiety disorders. Although we have explained the benefits of aerobic activity in stress reduction, there are many other forms of stress reduction, such as Tai Chi, meditation, yoga, breath work, biofeedback, progressive muscle relaxation (PMR), visualization, impulsivity inhibition, stop and think, time-out, and others that can be employed in a number of circumstances. These and other stress-reduction and relaxation methods can be found in a variety of stress-management and relaxation books.

6
Modeling Self-Esteem and Success

Modeling has been recognized as one of the most powerful means of initiating healthy behavioral changes. Adventure-based counseling presents a special opportunity for the counselor to model healthy behavior for the client. For vulnerable kids to see healthy adult friends (I use the word "friend," because I believe it is important for the counselor to have established this relationship) falter, handle it with grace, and continue is powerful therapy. The stage can be set for us to fall as we skate, laugh at our mistakes or clumsiness, and to get back up and skate, however timidly. This can also be accomplished by missing when shooting baskets, tipping over a canoe, falling on the ski trail, missing the target in archery, etc. Usually, such miscues are more spontaneous and not staged, which requires a healthy level of self-control and a good sense of humor on the part of the therapist.

Although a good adventure-based counselor must be able to make sacrifices, falling from or off a ropes course is not advised. The attempt here is not to appear to be an absolute klutz or reckless, but rather to show kids that it's okay to participate in something with which they may have difficulty, and that it's okay to make mistakes. Taking on new challenges is a necessary step in becoming competent. We want to encourage hesitant children, especially those who have grown up with failure, to take on new, healthy challenges.

When people (young and old) stop challenging themselves, they stop growing. Many of these children are already behind physically, as well as socially and emotionally. When they experience success and feel good about taking on new challenges, they feel better about themselves and become more ready for the outside world.

Helping Shawn Face His Fear of Bicycling — A Case Study

Shawn had several unusual fears. One of them was riding a bike. His impulsive and inappropriate behavior isolated him from normal peer relations. Due to several early childhood concerns, his mother often discouraged participation in activities that could be challenging and/or cause physical pain. Shawn's early fears were validated by his mother's need to protect him from any further painful events. When Shawn was invited to join another client and therapist on a mountain bike ride, he had to decline, but to save face he said that he didn't like mountain biking. It was obvious that Shawn felt a sense of failure, failure not only in biking but also in his to attempt to establish a new friendship. The therapist's impression was that Shawn would not be capable of directly addressing the fear because of his lack of self-worth. Furthermore, the overriding defensiveness prevented him from recognizing his needs. Shawn needed help in order to feel better about himself and about facing and working through his inadequacies. Because he had previously experienced success at the ropes course, the therapist returned to the course where he and Shawn set new goals. This made Shawn feel better about himself. The experience reduced Shawn's defensiveness and provided the therapist with an opportunity to talk about his inability to ride a bicycle, while he still felt good about his accomplishments on the ropes course. By helping Shawn to recognize his successes and strengths and the good feelings he experienced with the new successes, the counselor helped Shawn acknowledge that learning to ride a bike can also bring new joy, and that the support he needed to learn would be there for him. Shawn needed to know that it was safe both physically and emotionally. The plan for the next session was a 20-minute office talk time, 20 minutes of trying a new challenge (biking), and 20 minutes with his activity of choice, which would give Shawn a successful close to the session. The biking success came early, and Shawn wanted to continue and do the trails that his friend Jimmy had done the week before. The therapist was so impressed with Shawn's success that he gave an exuberant "let's go," and off they went. However, by the time they had hit their fourth off-road uphill, Shawn was exhausted, hating biking and, at that point, not liking his therapist very much either. After reaching a "special landmark," they headed back. Shawn had difficulty with the terrain and the distance. He was joyous with his accomplishment until his mother drove in the driveway. Shawn described the trip to his mother as a life-

threatening, physically impossible ride, and said he didn't want to ever do it again. Shawn had dumped the anger of his discomfort on his mother who had always accepted her son's stress by coming to his aid. Mom was his safe target. However, Shawn signed up for a group trip a couple of weeks later, which featured two hours of mountain biking and two hours of rock-climbing. The success, experience and positive reinforcement provided enough initiative for Shawn to want to bike again.

Through this experience, Shawn learned perseverance. Mom, who was often dealing with her own pains of separation and reduced nurturing, learned the importance of letting go, and the therapist learned that we need to keep in check the level of early success and the degree of potential overload. It is generally best to keep both the level of success and the desire to return to a healthy activity at a high.

It is important for the therapist not to get so caught up into the challenge that he loses sight of the degree of accomplishment necessary to be therapeutically beneficial, or that therapy embraces the value of learning not only to cope, but also to value one's accomplishments, even though they may fall short of one's goals. It is essential to encourage the child to continue beyond that point of fear and frustration. It is essential in order to help the child develop healthy new ways of being in the world and to let go of the fear and the reluctance to try.

If a child never rides a bike, for instance, consider the social and emotional ramifications of feeling left out in a world of bicycle-riding peers. Children need healthy exposure, and, as counselors, we need to help eliminate the fear, or at least try to reduce it. If the child doesn't get on the bike, he cannot learn to ride. If the child stays away from water, he cannot learn to swim. If the child doesn't go to the mountains, he cannot learn to ski or to hike in rugged terrain. Helping parents to teach proper modeling techniques and nonconfrontative encouragement, complimented by some rational decision-making, are also essential components of a multi-pronged therapeutic approach. We, as counselors and educators, can help open the doors to new and healthy life experiences.

Parents often need help in understanding, working and playing with their children. The adventure-based counselor can help the parents to model participation in a variety of activities with their child and through role plays. The therapist must be emphatic and firm in teaching the parents to persevere, to try, fail, try, and ultimately succeed. Success can be controlled in the therapeutic setting, but, in the real world the highway to success must pass through unanticipated failures. Helping the parents to help the child by allowing him to try, to fail, to persevere, to succeed, and to be encouraged through approval is crucial in the therapeutic process.

Parent Modeling

Parental modeling is critical in helping the child to develop positive behaviors. Parents often need assistance to change years of their nonproductive behaviors in order to model healthy behavior for their child.

It is helpful for the counselor to assess the parents' level of self-worth to determine where to begin to develop their appreciation for and recognition and understanding of the importance such modeling plays in the development of their child's self-esteem. A parent whose self-worth is low generally is ill-equipped to provide positive modeling. Parents need to see themselves as worthy and essential to the positive development of their children. The old adage of "do as I say, not as I do" holds little credibility in this day and age. As the parents' self-worth and self-confidence improve, they can learn to be less defensive and to respond more positively to their children. The therapist will generally have greater contact with a child's parents than with an adolescent's parents, however, both deserve the help to become more confident in providing for their child. The teaming approach (supporting one another for the sake of the child), whether the parents are married, separated, or divorced, is critical in the cognitive and emotional development of the child. Under these circumstances, the parents can provide for a more enriched developmental setting. Parents should be given ideas appropriate to their circumstances, and the counselor might find it more effective to model these parenting skills for them. This may involve contracts, especially for parents who are separated or divorced.

Parent-group sessions also allow parents to share their trials and successes and to see that they are not alone. Support groups foster a special camaraderie among parents. Adventure-based programming can be a powerful addition to support groups. Parents can see and feel their child's struggles and successes. Parents can relate to and support one another.

The following list provides a few modeling techniques, examples and provisions for parents to use in helping to improve their child's self-confidence and self-concept.

- Be able to say "I'm sorry." This, of course, first requires the parent to admit that he or she is capable of being wrong. If the parent is never wrong, the chances are the child will never be wrong either. This I'm-never-wrong attitude could present quite a challenge when the child becomes 15 or 16. In order to recognize the value of positive reflective insight, the parent might try to look at the world through the eyes of his child. Really listening to the child without plotting what to say next, particularly if the child is trying to explain or to negotiate something with the parent, the insight could be significant. If the escalation of emotions has already begun, parents should take an unconditional, nonjudgmental time-out (usually 15 minutes to an hour or more) to allow both sides time to become emotionally collected enough to talk and think rationally (a walk, run, bike, or comparable exercise is recommended). Trying to prove that the other is at fault in the crisis is not effective. Fault is not the point. Parents must learn that listening, understanding, and compromising are essential to a satisfactory interaction.

- Accept responsibility for their own shortcomings/actions. Too often, (more often for those already feeling stress or suffering from low self-esteem) parents will immediately blame the child for an error they made. "The reason I spilled your milk is because you didn't finish it, and the reason I backed into your mother's car is because you made me late so I had to rush. If a parent can't take responsibility for the situation, then he can't expect his child to take responsibility for the shared or individual actions, now or in the future. It is not likely that after Dad runs over his son's bike and yells at him for leaving it in the driveway that the child is going to say, "Okay, Dad, thanks! I've learned my lesson!" The lesson he learns is not likely to be the one that Dad, in a rage, hopes he will learn.

- Encourage parents to say, "I love you!" These words are powerful and reassuring.

- Encourage the parents to play with their child without passing judgment. A little coaching goes a long way, and a lot of coaching goes nowhere. Most children don't want to be coached and judged by their parents: they just want to play with their parents in a nonjudgmental way. They want parental acceptance. Family adventure-based sessions have been very helpful here.

- Understand the priorities in the child's life. This concept may, in itself, necessitate some help from the counselor. It is good to find out how the parent thinks he/she will view the amount and the quality of time spent with the child in the future, say in 10 years. If the counselor can help the parent to see that the time with the child is an investment in the child's future, the parent may more readily understand the value of playing and spending quality time with the child. Having parents listen to the song *Cats in the Cradle* during a session offers a good object lesson. The story line is about a father who has many excuses, all of them good ones, for not spending time with his son — too many responsibilities, having to be out of town earning a living. He tells the son that they will get together soon and "we'll have a good time then." The story comes full circle. The aging father wonders why his son never comes to visit him, and he hears the same excuses he gave. Like the father, the son says that they will get together soon and have a good time then. Talking with parents about what they hear in the words of the song will help them to understand that the time they invest in their children, the priorities they set now, help to determine how the child learns to set priorities. Parents should be praised well for their positive interaction with their children.

- Encourage parents to stay physically active and to eat well. Parents who feel better, generally perform better.

- Encourage parents to let the child in them out everyday. A little bit of the child we were exists in most of us. Adults frequently have the idea that they should not have child-like fun and joy. If parents can learn to enjoy the child that lives in them and to permit the child to come out, they will better understand the child who comes to them for guidance.

- Encourage parents to show random acts of kindness in front of their children. This is modeling of the most positive kind. Encourage them to do such things as letting someone cut in front of them in line at the supermarket, or make room for another car to edge into traffic in front of them. Anything that shows that "giving in" in such situations shows control and strength, not weakness.

- Help parents to understand the value of compassion. A parent who shows compassion for the suffering or the misfortunes of another human being, especially those of his child, provides a strong object lesson: taking a moment to help someone or to talk caringly with that person is another demonstration of strength of character. The parent who expresses true compassion for his child's difficult day at school, or for the unkind words of the child's peers, underscores the idea that expressing words of kindness and true concern is not a show of weakness.

- Encourage the parent to reach out to someone who is less fortunate. The parent who reaches out to someone in unfortunate circumstances helps the child to put his problems into perspective. This is especially true when the parent talks with the child about this act of kindness and compassion. Being beaten up on the playground might make a bummer of a day, but helping someone who is without food or adequate clothing can put the events of the day in a different perspective.

- Remind the parent to model honesty and trust. The $2 a parent saves at the movies by passing his 13-year-old child off as a 12-year-old, for instance, could prove to have a short-term gain and a long-term loss. Such displays of dishonesty and betrayal of trust will become part of the child's value system.

It should be noted that in this list of modeling, three of the top five items are qualities that kids like most in their friends (as researched through *Adventurelore* programs in more than 1,000 children): caring, trust, and communication. When parents and therapists help children establish and maintain these qualities, the emphasis goes a long way in helping the children to feel good about themselves and their peer relations, which is so critical in child and adolescent development.

Real-Life Modeling Adventurelore Style — Case Studies

Case 1: A close friend and associate of mine, Dr. John Yeager, was helping to lead a canoe group in one of Maine's gorgeous rivers. The canoes were unloaded from the trailer and placed in the water. The paddles were appropriately sized and distributed to the canoeists. As Dr. John stepped into the canoe to demonstrate a technique, he was a little off balance, and it flipped over like a dog with fleas. Dr. John, in a moment, became Captain Capsize. A key therapeutic benefit was achieved when, by the time his head popped up, he was smiling and the children's fear was released. The Captain's lesson on canoeing was enhanced by his positive reaction to a situation that could have been perceived as stressful.

"Captain Capsize"

Case 2: I took a group of children on our annual two-day ski trip. On the last run of the day, I decided to try, as did the better skiers before me, to glide over a three-foot deep, 20-yard long pool of water at the bottom of the slope. Apparently, I was lacking in speed as I hit the water. I completed 10 of the 20 yards needed to get across. My skis dipped and stopped — I continued. I surfaced to the booming applause of onlookers, and then took a bow. The children enjoyed the humor of the challenging moment. Several felt safe enough to challenge the winter water trap and had greater success than I, thankfully. It is important to note that it was the last run of the day and a change of dry clothes was quickly available. Kids need to be equally able to distinguish between healthy challenges and foolish challenges.

These two cases of modeling, however real, are of a more grandiose level. Often modeling is as simple as saying "thank you" or "good shot" or "good game" or laughing with the child when he exercises appropriate humor. Another excellent example of modeling is to regain a positive attitude and not overreact when things go wrong.

When working in a two-to-two therapeutic setting (two counselors, two clients) on the basketball court, the stage is set for the therapists to compliment each other on a good play or good attempts. A great opportunity to model sportsmanship is to demonstrate honesty on a close call and to give and receive praise for honesty (i.e., good call, thank you, exchanging high five's). Success is also reinforced when the clients use team work in their play. "Jimmy, that was a great pass. You guys are a great team!"

It's very helpful to process feelings and attitudes and to reinforce positive behaviors exhibited during small groups. In the closure of a session, it is important to discuss how those behaviors can carry over into a school or home environment. The time spent on this transference process is generally time well spent. In addition to discussing and illustrating the therapy-based behaviors and the integration of those behaviors at school and home, it is important to communicate with and assist the school personnel and parents who are involved with that particular child. The coordination of efforts among the three domains, (home, school, and therapeutic) help to reinforce the transference of healthy social and emotional behaviors. This communication may be accomplished by periodic meetings, phone contact, and/or in writing. Generally, I prefer the first two because they allow for immediate feedback and a greater potential for a more complete understanding and a better exchange of ideas.

Modeling may involve positive reactions to small accidents or difficulties (e.g., having your glasses fall in the mud, spilling a drink on the floor and not overreacting). In short, this modeling teaches children to smile through their difficulties and teaches them techniques that foster a quicker recovery from difficult times. It's hard to stay upset when you're smiling. It's hard to stay angry at someone when you are holding hands. Modeling these behaviors as well as incorporating role plays, helps children and adults alike to develop a healthier control system and positive demeanor when encountering challenging situations. Kids and adults both need to recognize and to understand that by taking control of their angers, big and small, they can reduce their anxiety and tension levels and deal with the issue much more effectively. Adventure based-counseling and appropriate processing of the experience helps to bring this to light.

Self-Disclosure

Self-disclosure, such as sharing some of your own difficulties as a child, allows the child to see you as human and provides some similar ground to share. This technique should not, of course, be used when a child needs recognition and validation of his feelings. An open ear and an empathetic, insight-stimulating approach is often the first direction. Common sense and some caution (stop and think) needs to be exercised during self-disclosure, and some counselors may feel more comfortable with it than others. To discuss a learning problem, organizational or impulsive disorder, or a family difficulty that the counselor experienced growing up may help the client relate to him as one who will better accept and understand him. Interpreting a story of how you or someone else you worked with successfully dealt with difficulty can bring possible solutions to some of life's problems. One needs to recognize clearly, however, when the child's troubles should not be minimized but recognized and paid the utmost attention. Make use of the most basic counseling skills: listen, reinforce, and listen.

Use common sense. For a counselor to report that he drank and smoked his way through college, stole his neighbor's car, had reckless sex, never did his homework, and went around breaking street lights establishes as little therapeutic credibility as teaching the child to swim with cement water wings. As a therapist, particularly one in an adventure-based practice, you are a model. As you were, so may your client wish to be.

7
The Counselor as a Person: Integrating Theories With Action*

Before we can begin to work with others as helpers, we must ourselves be healthy in body, mind, and spirit. Counselor education that requires personal qualities and skills cannot be overlaid on emotional chaos and identity confusion.

I like what George Shehan, the great writer on physical and psychological health said in a talk at the University of New Hampshire, "First be a good animal." He emphasized that if we are dull and sluggish in our physical domain, we will not have optimal mental clarity. Obviously, our ability to respond effectively depends upon our sense of well-being, which means we need to be relatively free from emotional turmoil. This is not to say that counselors are impervious to distress. It simply means that our own psychosocial issues should not get in the way of our being competent in our professional relationships and responsibilities.

It is important that we maintain a high degree of awareness and balanced perspective about our physical, mental, social, emotional, and spiritual dimensions, and the ability to express this healthy integration of our wholeness. This is what we want for our clients. As counselors, we should not ask less of ourselves. We have to walk the walk, not just talk the talk.

Ongoing Professional Development

If there is to be real professional development, it also will be personal development. There must be an integration of skills, techniques, interventions, knowledge, systems, and theories in the person who will manifest these.

---

*Developed by Dwight Webb, Ph.D., Staff Psychologist, Adventurelore.

Our first imperative is to do no harm, but we must set the sights of our professional development much higher, with vision and optimism. We want our staff to communicate that we see the good and that which is possible in people, even though their struggles cloud their dreams and may temporarily obscure their path. Our bedrock philosophy is believing in and having faith in our clients as whole and decent persons worthy of respect. Our staff development is a continuous process in collegial debriefing and ongoing supervision in every aspect of their work.

We ask our staff members to be fully aware of and accountable to our principles and processes and to continue to hone their knowledge and skills of the latest and best that is known in our field.

Seeing the Client in Context

As our work with clients unfolds, our focus must be beyond our immediate appointment in such a way that today's interventions and therapeutic designs fit into an overall scheme, aimed at both short- and long-term goals. This requires an intuitive awareness of the context, the flow, and the barriers to our clients most desirable development. In our staff development, we encourage the counselor to call upon their own intuition because it incorporates sensing and sensitivity and leaves room for a willingness to abandon treatment schedules, techniques, or systems that may turn out to be inappropriate, given the immediate circumstances with the client. Being intuitive means being highly aware of the here and now and being flexible, as well as spontaneous and creative.

Building Rapport: The Golden Key to Relationships

Relationships, if they are going to be mutual and growthful, start with establishing and maintaining rapport. Rapport is the bridge between people that creates an easy flow of communication. It opens the human spirit to warmth and laughter, to tears, and to quiet support. Rapport may be expressed in tones of voice and in posture, as well as with eye contact and words. When there is true rapport, there is an ease between people.

Rapport is fundamental to trust. Doing activities without trust is like running a machine without oil; it's going to seize up and stop running. While it is true that the facilitator must have great technical skill in conducting adventure-based exercises, all the technique in the world will be of little use if there is no rapport in his or her relationship with the client.

The personal characteristics coming from the counselor must carry a message that says, "I believe in you and your inner power to become, to grow, to transcend." It is the person of the counselor who by his or her faith in the goodness and the potential of their client creates an atmosphere and a climate in which growth and change are most likely to flower.

Briefing and Framing the Plan

As facilitators, we have a responsibility to be effective communicators, to be clear, to be heard, and to be understood. Clients need to be invited and challenged to be open to learning and not just to have a "Wow, wasn't that fun" experience.

Counselors must themselves be able to conceptualize the wholeness of the therapeutic experience — the flow from the beginning, to the middle, and to the conclusion of activities, through to the importance of learner integration and transfer. The briefing needs to be both specific and vague. Specific in the instructions for conducting the activity and initiating process events, and vague in terms of not revealing the purposes or outcomes that need to be discovered by participants if learning is to be fully claimed.

Genuine Enthusiasm

The spirit of enthusiasm in the counselor is an important fundamental, personal characteristic. This kind of up-beat attitude must be genuine, and keeping this edge requires all the discipline of a virtuoso musician. The difference is, the counselor is the instrument and the player. Our balance, texture, humor, warmth, and sincerity all need to resonate in fullness and harmony, or what Carl Rogers speaks of as congruence. He defines congruence as being that experience when what we are saying, feeling, and thinking all come together as one clear and whole message. When we are well-integrated, our level of genuineness is transparent, and our natural caring and vitality will be manifest. Throughout all adventure activities, the counselor must consistently communicate that clients will be safe, and they will be supported and listened to. While they will be encouraged to try new challenges, they will always be respected and have the freedom to choose their level of participation.

Processing the Experience: Bringing Meaning to New Ways of Being

This is a key element in the adventure process and the time when clients experience their greatest learning and integration. It is in processing that transfers are discovered and when participants are most open to changing their behavior. Because adventure-based activities are so much fun and the challenge so exciting, there may be a tendency to cut short the processing. This would be a mistake. Although the counselor may place major importance on the adventure experience itself initially, understanding the implications of what occurred will enhance the impact and meaning in the client's daily life. Processing illuminates the personal meaning for the clients.

Theories in Action — An Integrative Example

Jennifer at the Climbing Wall

Jennifer is a bright 17-year-old high school drop-out who is angry about her parents recent divorce. This is her fourth individual session, with Trish, her counselor. They are standing in front of the climbing wall. Jennifer is staring at the wall. A barrier, looming in front of her.

"Damn! This doesn't look safe! I might fall! I'm not strong enough to climb and hold onto those little nubs. Forget it! I'm not ready for this challenge!"

Then she says to herself . . .

It must be do-able. There must be a way. I'm going to look like a fool if I don't at least try. Where is my self-respect? Come on, try. You can do it.

Internally, she is experiencing fear, embarrassment, and self-judgment. These different voices play out as follows:

Physically: I might get hurt.

Socially: I'll look like a fool if I fail, or I'll look like a coward if I don't try.

Psychologically: I will lose self-respect if I don't try.

Trish is tuned in, sensing Jennifer's resistance and acknowledges it. This is a tough one, kind of scary! She shows respect for Jennifer and her feelings and then wonders to herself, "What does she need right now? I want to encourage her but don't want to rush in and fix things." Trish decides, "I'm going to leave her alone to struggle with her decision for a moment, let her live with her dilemma and choices, let her be with her feelings. OK, gentle encouragement here, with challenge." Then Trish says out loud, "I think you can do it." Trish is expressing:

Respect: Letting Jennifer decide

Support: Acknowledging difficulty

Challenge: Giving encouragement

At this point, Jennifer will choose. She will either decide to try it, or she will decide not to try. It's a critical decision, and it's all hers. Trish will support either decision, and that's very important for Jennifer to know. There is a long pause, Jennifer stares up at the challenge before her, then says, "I'll try it." Scared, but resolved, she starts out. Trish has Jennifer on belay and tells her she is safe. Jennifer knows this because she's been on belay before, on an easier activity, and has actually fallen with Trish there to catch her. Jennifer's only surprise was how soft the catch felt. It was totally comfortable.

This time it is different. Her fear is controlled by her experience and her belief that humans don't climb vertical walls. Jennifer grabs and steps on the first reachable outcrop and lifts herself up, deciding not to look down, she pushes with her legs, pulling with her arms for support and for holding. She asks Trish which way to go next. Trish answers with encouragement and invites her to explore her options. She tells Jennifer that she is doing great, to take a few deep breaths and relax, that she's right on top of it. Jennifer moves like a spider woman. She is strong and getting stronger, and, with each step, more confident. She reaches the top of the wall, and lets out a "Hooray! I did it!" This was such a powerful success, with her jubilance in sharp contrast to the paralyzing fear she experienced just minutes before.

After the rappel (piece of cake), Trish sits down with Jennifer and asks: Trish: What did you learn?

Jennifer: That I can do things I didn't think I could.

Trish: Uh huh! Anything else?

Jennifer: That sometimes I'm too timid and try to play it safe.

Trish: How do you feel about that?

Jennifer: I want to break that pattern, try new things, take more risks.

Trish: Yes. (affirming) You sound real clear about that. (acknowledging) "Can you think of any examples of how this might translate into your day-to-day life situations?

75

Jennifer: Well, (pause) Yes. I dropped out of school because I was afraid to try (pause). I think now I can (pause) no let me change that. I know now that I can do it if I put my mind to it.

Trish: Great! Anything else?

Jennifer: Yes. That I can ask for help. That I can trust other people. When I was on the wall, it was great knowing you were there for me if I fell.

Trish: How might that be in other situations?

Jennifer: I guess there are lots of people out there willing to help me if I ask, and if I let them.

Throughout this dialogue, we see Trish communicating respect, support, and challenge as she invites Jennifer to review and to discover her own meanings.

Seeing that Theories Are Not Isolated from Each Other

Theories are tools. They are the distilled ideas of our best thinkers and researchers in the social sciences. They speak of principles that, when applied under certain conditions, will produce predictable results. But theories are not fact, nor are they discrete building blocks, and standing alone they do not apply to all situations for all people.

Trish has had training in all the major theories of counseling, and, in this vignette, she is incorporating and manifesting the principles of several theories without planning or monitoring them. She is in the flow of interaction, being totally immersed in the context of the moment and her part in it. She has integrated theoretical models into her way of being.

Here are some of the major ideas from current dominant theories of counseling that might be brought to bear in such an interaction. These principles are emphasized to demonstrate the breadth and the interweaving of some possible applications in adventure-based counseling.

Existential-Humanistic
- Believes in the person's internal frame of reference and subjective experience.
- Confronts self-determination and personal responsibility.
- Chooses experiences to create an opportunity to change, to re-invent one's being.
- Finds meaning in all experience, in adversity, and in blessings.

- Demands response to anxiety and is often the impetus for personal growth.
- Focuses on authenticity, because being true to one's self will lead to integration.
- Fosters freedom to choose an attitude about any given set of circumstances.

Person-Centered

- Human beings tend to move toward wholeness and self-actualization.
- Individuals and groups will find their own direction with a minimum degree of help from the facilitator.
- Personal qualities of the helping person are more important than techniques.
- A primary function of the counselor is to create a climate that is psychologically safe. Such a climate is established by creating relationships based on attitudes and behaviors that demonstrate empathy, acceptance, unconditional positive regard, warmth, caring, respect, genuineness, immediacy, and the freedom to choose their level of participation.

Behavioral

- Behavior is learned and can be unlearned.
- Learning has strong stimulus/response bonding.
- Behaviors that are reinforced get repeated.
- Teaching assertiveness skills helps identify specific behavior that will be reinforced.
- Evaluation and accountability are essential.
- Goals are defined in concrete behavioral terms, which can be observed and measured.
- Rehearsal encourages new behaviors to be tried and reinforced with constructive feedback.
- Modeling can provide examples of positive behavior that may be imitated and help clients to explore options for more healthy coping.
- Visual imagery and relaxation training stimulate imagination and provide successful fantasy rehearsal for problem solving, which will benefit later real life challenges.
- Although the emphasis is on objectivity, there must be trust, patience, warmth, and other human qualities in the relationship if there is to be cooperation.

Cognitive

- We filter and interpret our experience through our belief system.

- Counselors challenge clients to learn to identify irrational beliefs that distort reality and impede performance.
- Primary emphasis is on the counselors skill and willingness to challenge, confront, probe, and persuade the client to practice activities that will lead to constructive new behaviors and belief systems (attitudes).

Gestalt Theory

- Awareness as to how behaviors, emotions, and belief systems interface is seen as fundamental to behavior change. Thus, clients need to see how their choices and their behavior patterns may influence their relationships and performance outcomes.
- The counselor's focus is on the here and now of the clients experience.
- The basic goal of the counselor is to challenge participants to become aware of how they are avoiding responsibility and to encourage them to look for internal support, rather than external support.

Reality Therapy

- Stresses personal responsibility.
- Teaches clients better ways to fulfill their needs, helping them to find more satisfactory behaviors that will lead to a "success" identity.
- Does not look for unconscious conflicts or the reasons for them. Clients may not excuse their behavior on the bases of unconscious motivation.
- Works in the present toward the future, refusing to accept the excuse that a person is limited by their past.
- Believes that in order to feel worthwhile, we need to *act* worthwhile.

Closing Remarks

Integration, openness, flexibility, thoughtful action, sensitivity, awareness, and humility are words that come to mind as I reflect on the complexity of providing a helpful relationship for another person. Call it counseling or therapy, facilitation or education, call it caring, or challenge and support, the point is beyond labeling and categorizing, emerging more from the quality of the human spirit in the caregiver.

Adventure activities provide the structure to create conditions wherein those who will come to learn and to grow may find a welcoming opportunity and a well-integrated and dependable guide to illuminate the path.

8
Adventure-Based Counseling and the Family

The inclusion of the family in adventure-based counseling allows the experiences to come alive and provides a powerful climate to address inhibiting and debilitating issues. The child or adolescent in counseling is commonly not the only one in the family with an unwelcome anxiety or emotional needs. Families with a member or members in need will benefit from developing a greater understanding of each other and developing more compassion for one another.

The ropes course, challenge wall, wall climb, and/or a variety of group initiatives provide a medium in which to practice and to experience giving and receiving support from one another. Both the ropes course and the climbing wall provide family members with an opportunity to verbally support and encourage others in their challenge. Trust is enhanced as one family member belays for another. Communication skills are strengthened through the use of a group initiative, such as the wall scale, the Board Walk, the Acid Swamp, or the Tire Tree. Each activity requires trust and communication to be successful. The family experiences the need for a trusting, open, and caring environment to be successful just as an athletic team or a friendship. A family needs to learn the value of having fun together, and they need to know how to play. The trampoline has been effective in helping families lighten up and experience joy and laughter together.

The post-activity processing focuses on recognition of success, the value of support systems, trust, communications, and how those systems can be implemented at home. Family members have had an opportunity to show support during activity-based therapy and need to recognize their role in supporting other family members to reduce their anxiety in other settings. Families need to know that there is a fine line between being empathic and being firmly supportive. Better still, families who learn how to carefully integrate the two will be more successful. Family members need to know the difference between being an enabler and being sensitive to the affected member's needs. The patience, understanding, and firm support of family members is critical to a healthy recovery.

The processing of such a session is a powerful tool in the development of the understanding of how the family is functioning and how it can function better. There needs to be discussion of what worked, what didn't work, and how clear the communication was. Did everyone get a chance to express their opinions and or needs? Were the opinions recognized and valued? What made the individual feel good? How does the individual feel now? How does the experience apply to life outside of counseling?

As a family, the individuals need to know that they must work together, play together, support one another, and understand that each family member has his own strengths and vulnerabilities. When we recognize those strengths and support one's efforts to strengthen against the vulnerabilities, the family will benefit as a whole. We all want to live in a healthy family environment, and we all need to cherish and to practice the role that we have in it. The adventure-based counselor can assist the family in developing a healthy structure by providing a means in which the individuals show and experience support, trust, and good communication.

The Board Walk

One of the many advantages of adventure-based counseling for the family is that it allows the counselor to observe and to point out how different interpersonal relationships play out in a structured activity. These group initiatives are designed to metaphorically represent the daily activities and challenges of living together and sharing the same goals and space with those around us. To be successful at the initiatives, group members must look at, struggle with, and implement powerful concepts, such as communication, cooperation, trust, and problem-solving. Perhaps the most beneficial result that will grow with activities such as these is the laughter and the fun that a family will experience and rediscover as the individuals share with one another.

A Case Study*

The Smiths, a family of four, had been bringing Joe to counseling on a weekly basis to work through the difficulties he was having at school. Joe was 14 years old and struggling with social, behavioral, and academic issues. After some initial work, it became apparent that much of what was on Joe's mind was related to his family. Saying good-bye to his older brother as he went off to college was turning out to be a painful loss for Joe. Not only was he losing the daily interac-

---

*Developed by Michael Volpe, M.Ed., *Adventurelore* counselor.

tion with a much admired and successful individual, but he also was left to deal with the family on his own. The focus would now turn from Brian and his achievements to Joe and everything he was messing up. After understanding some initial family dynamics, it was agreed that we would try some family counseling, incorporating adventure-based counseling techniques.

The family selected the Board Walk for their initial experience. The goal of this basic challenge is to transport the members of the group from one end of the field to the other end (about 25 yards) without touching the ground (see page 106). If any part of the body comes in contact with the ground, the person must return to the starting line. Each group member is given a board that measures one square foot and instructed to use it to achieve their goal.

The first attempt was clearly everyone for themselves, with Dad out in front. Joe was quite a way behind, and Mom was still at the starting line, unable to go too far. After some talk of cooperation, how it feels to be last instead of in control, and restating the original goal, we started again. This time, the three of them began to understand that by working together they were able to move in a line down the field, at a slower but more consistent rate. There emerged, however, some entirely new challenges. This time trust and touch and sharing were integral parts of the process. It was interesting to note how many family issues could be talked about in terms of these concepts. It was even more interesting to discuss just how difficult it is for us to deal with these ideas.

As the activity progressed, the frustration inherent in the task brought about the sarcastic and sharp side of Dad. After falling off the boards a couple of times, Dad became so frustrated that his best response was to kick the board and exclaim, "son of a bitch!" After returning to the starting line, which was also now in the back of the progression, Dad began to settle in and get serious. Here he had to function from a position of need, instead of control. This was a new role for Dad and an important issue to look at later. Also important to process later is the idea that we all have many stressors in our lives that will fuel our sarcastic and sharp side. How we deal with them is what makes the difference in our life and the lives we touch. It was beginning to become clear to the whole family that this was not just a silly game in the woods.

It becomes hard for a family to function when individuals are not in their typical roles. In this case, with Dad in the back, without the ability to move on by himself, the next move for any of them was unclear. Rather than deal with this responsibility and take advantage of the opportunity to boost Dad's ego and win favor, Joe decides to fake a fall. This accomplishes two of Joe's strongest desires: to be like Dad and never be noticed as being better at something than Dad is. Now, back at the beginning with his Dad, Joe reconstructs the family as it functions, i.e., Mom apart from the men, and Joe with yet another chance to earn approval from his Dad. So with the positions realigned Dad is happy again. As he moves along, he exclaims "We'll make it buddy!" and "That a boy!" Eventually the men connect with Mom, and the business of crossing the field is again at hand.

As the group began the process, so did our opportunity to look at how communication, both verbal and non-verbal, works with this family. It became clearer how the Smiths made decisions, asked for help, shared ideas, and generally interacted together. Any and all of the comments that were taking place would soon be eligible for discussion in the processing sessions after this activity.

How a family works together also will be illuminated in an activity like this. The support that is offered in the physical realm, such as holding on to or lifting someone parallels the emotional support that exists in family relationships. Watching when and how each member of the Smith family supported another and the group as a whole during the activity helped the counselor to understand and later to discuss how they exist for each other. The Smiths began to understand that in order to be successful in this activity and in life they must work together, offer and accept support, and use the strengths of one another.

As the group continued it's journey, each person discovered, as Dad had earlier, that dealing and coping with different frustrations and difficulties was what this activity was all about. In fact, as soon as the Smiths began to excel at the activity under the existing parameters, we changed the requirements. Some of the minor adjustments that can be made in a game like the Board Walk were implemented here. To begin with, the group was limited to two boards instead of three, and Dad was chosen to participate blindfolded. As the Smiths complained about the fairness of this treatment, the question of how they as a family deal with set backs and irritations arose. How do we as individuals respond to aggravating people or terrible situations? How do we cope with our limitations and an unfair turn of events? It was important for the Smiths to take a break and to talk about the value of "making lemonade when life gives you lemons," and how we must all "play the hands we are dealt." This family would need to improvise, adapt, and overcome the challenges put to them. Dad, especially, would need to rely on his other senses, different strengths, and the most crucial people in his life. Mom and Joe would have to rise to the occasion and concentrate even more on the communication and the cooperation among the family that day. Feelings of embarrassment, fear, and foolishness had to be set aside and an attitude of persistence and perseverance needed to surface. The family continued this wonderful and strange trip.

The Smiths, faced with new rules and boundaries, had similar reactions and responses to other groups in this circumstance. They had their ups and downs and were not afraid to get into it with each other or the counselor. Something about the woods seems to lower typical inhibitions. Most importantly, however, was that, at the end of it all, the Smiths laughed. They left counseling that day with stories of a crazy game that allowed them to enjoy each other. We often, in our busy lives, forget to enjoy those around us. We forget to embrace life's delicious ambiguities. The Smiths, above all else, had fun together. It is what they longed for. It was what was missing.

The sessions that followed this day in the woods were filled with discussions about what had transpired as the family faced the Board Walk. We talked about how each and every action and reaction that took place during the game could be thought about in terms of their lives and adjusted to make things better. How the Smiths treated one another and dealt with the activity was a picture of what happens at the Smith household. They could begin to see some issues that needed to be addressed. It was our job to do so now. This adventure-based activity was an initial step in the process of taking back (their) lives.

Helping the parents to set the stage for their child's involvement in these activities is an important step in the child's therapy. A very important long-term therapeutic purpose is to expose the child to a variety of fun and healthy activities so he will be more likely to continue the activities in his home or school environment. An activity that is fun for one person, however, may not be fun for another. Therapists should encourage nonjudgmental fun play between parents and their children to enhance the likelihood of further healthy physical interaction between parent and child. The stress release is often as important for the parent as it is for the child. Another factor (not aerobically related) is that fun activities between parent and child help enhance parent/child communication. There is a creation of a common bond that is fun, a very positive experience and further discussion of it will likely be positive, thus we have communication.

Islands of Communication

Too often parents get into the rut of dominating the parent-child communication with conversation that is judgmental and/or challenging. Such as: "Is your homework done," "Who are you on the phone with now?" "Do you know you left a mess in the kitchen last night?" "Your room is a pig pen!" All of these comments inhibit communication between parent and child and closes the door to good rapport. Certainly some (or all) of these issues need to be addressed, however, if it becomes the main topic of conversation, young people will find a way to avoid communication and tune out.

Developing a number of pleasant and enjoyable experiences provides for conversation that is easy-flowing and more positive. Most families that play together talk together. By sharing enjoyable experiences, families develop a number of avenues of common interest and talk about them, thus improving the total parent-child relationship. As common interests and experiences expand, "islands of communication" develop, which fosters a more complete sense of communication to include positive experiences as well as enjoyable topics. Islands of communication bridge the gaps between kids and adults. Islands of communication are developed by doing healthy, fun activities (sports, recreation, hobbies, etc.) together.

Adventure-based counselors can be very instrumental in helping families participate in activities in which they all can join. The powerful learning is illuminated in the debriefing process as they examine the dynamics and the interfamily communications that have been displayed in this positive, adventure-based activity.

We have explained that involvement in an aerobic activity is generally more important in a parent/child activity than in a parent/adolescent relationship. This is not to say parent/adolescent physical relationships are not important. Indeed they are. However, the sooner the healthy behaviors are established, the better. By the age of 13 or 14, many adolescents have developed a fairly strong competency in their activity level. Their level of ability in aerobic-type activities may have already surpassed that of their parents, nonetheless for many, perhaps most, this is a very important time to share an interest in healthy activities. Skiing, biking, basketball, and tennis are common means to achieve these goals. Parents sometime need to be reminded, especially the competitive dads, that these activities are not do-or-die, all-or-nothing activities, with the winner becoming the dominant figure in the family setting. Play! Enjoy!

Win! Lose! Laugh! The goal is to model healthy behaviors, have fun, and promote a desire for continued joint activities. Many games and adventure challenges need not be a one-versus-the-other situation. In circumstances where healthy competitive games create more anxiety than fun, choose the more noncompetitive activities, such as biking, canoeing, hiking, catch, or even adapt traditionally more competitive games. For example, see how a parent and a child improve their combined shooting abilities in shooting baskets in a period of two minutes. This can reduce an overly competitive edge and enhance a mode of working together. See how long they, as a team, can continue a volley in either tennis or badminton. How many continuous catches can they make together with a ball, and how long can they continue to bounce a beach ball in the air. The teaming challenges are limited only as one's imagination is limited.

On a cold wintery afternoon I suggested to my two sons and one of their friends that we take a cross-country ski to Rock Rimmon, a small mountain through the woods from our home. They were quite comfortable inside playing a game, but were interested in having a snowball fight. The snowball fight wasn't high on my list of things to do; however, we negotiated a deal. We would ski to Rock Rimmon and have a snowball fight there. After the ski trip, we pelted one another with snowballs. I became snow beaten. For an hour, we laughed and played hard, as we wrestled each other in the snow and rolled down the side of the mountain. We had designed a plan for ourselves, with some compromise, to create an exceptionally fun-filled afternoon. We all got what we asked for and more. Communication about the event was abundant, and although I didn't get done what I had originally planned to do that day, the value of a nonjudgmental fun time with my sons was life at its best. We as counselors may need to teach parents how to play with their children. Parents need to learn to lighten up and have fun with their children. We need to help them become spontaneous. Parents should encourage adolescents to become physically active, whether it be in competitive or leisure-time sports. Enticing works better than pushing. Lead the way. The cooperation will vary from family to family, but jogging, walking, hiking, canoeing, soccer, football, swimming, bicycling, skiing, tennis, and basketball are just a few ideas.

Miscommunication

Some trust is lost in miscommunication, as is shown in this typical parent/child dialogue.

"You promised me! You said if I got a "C" average you would buy me a car!"

"I said if you got nothing lower than a C and your homework grades were all good, I'd let you use our car!"

85

Emotions begin to escalate and the cognitive process is impaired.

"That's not true!"

"Yes, it is true!"

"Now you're lying to me! I can't even trust my own parents. You're always going back on your word!"

"Don't you dare call me a liar! You told us you stayed after school to do make-up work, and we find out that you're downtown."

"See, you don't believe me! I stayed after but Mrs. Betts wasn't in so I went downtown to use a phone to call home!"

"Why didn't you call from school?"

"The phones were being used and . . ."

This very typical scenario is an example of how trust is compromised by poor communication. First and foremost, it is important for a parent to model trust, and, second, to communicate clearly. Those "deals" that are long-term (more than a day or two), especially if they have major significance to the child, are generally best written down, particularly if there is any history of miscommunication. This is not to discount trust in the family members but to secure intra-family communication. When trust is broken, it can ignite a chain reaction leading to significant parent/child conflict. The therapist first persuades the family that trust has a powerful influence upon the well-being of the family and that every family benefits substantially when the family trust is high. Each family member has an important role in the establishment of a trusting family relationship. To assist the family, we must help it to recognize the origin of the problem, to see the value of trust in the family, and to work as a team (without blame) to improve the situation.

During a family session, the adventure-based counselor may get a sense from family members where they feel trust has been important in their lives, where it has been compromised, how each felt, and how this impacts their sense of the value of trust. The implementation of an abbreviated Board Walk with blindfolds or Acid Swamp, (see Chapter 10), is helpful to develop an awareness of the value of trust in the family and the influence communication has on trusting. The ropes course or climbing wall will allow one family member to belay another during a difficult and emotionally heightened challenge. Other members offer their support, which provides a very powerful metaphor for trust and support. Each difficult grasp of the climbing wall or step on the ropes course is a metaphor for real-life challenges, and each slip and tug from the belayor is that support and trust so helpful in making it through difficult times to reach our goals. The experience makes the principles become bigger than life.

Debriefing with the Whole Family

To chat briefly about certain accomplishments and points of struggle helps provide an upbeat retrospect of the adventure experience and a discussion, appropriately led, in which the whole family can share. This, in turn, provides a base for communication. Questions that can help to pull the experience together and help in the transference to similar situations at home are:

- What was the scariest part of your challenge?
- How great was your level of trust at first?
- Did you ever feel complete trust? At what point?
- What helped you to gain trust?
- How was that trust different from trust at home?
- Are communications more or less clear under these circumstances than at home? How do they differ?
- Are the repercussions of breaking trust here more or less severe than at home?
- Can the elements of clarity used here be used at home? How do you feel they could be used?
- How did you feel when you were belaying _____ (another family member)?
- How does his trusting you with his life or well-being compare to the level of trust at home?
- What means of establishing and maintaining trust here can you use at home?
- What other forms of trust and communications do you feel would be helpful at home?

Although taking a lot of notes during a session can be inhibiting, notes are helpful to make the cognitive transfer focus directly on trust and communication. The questions offered above are only a guide in which to stimulate reflection and understanding, and to gain further insight as to how trust and communication impacts the whole family, and how it may evolve at home.

Role plays also are beneficial in helping the family to better understand the value of trust and communication. The therapist may use a number of sessions in order to give family members a chance to play different roles. This helps each person to develop greater insight into the positions of other members. Sometimes, shifting the focus to a fictional character, and circumstance can ease the level of hostility and defensiveness. The therapist must establish the parallels and reset the stage to learn how positive solutions are drawn from the role play and how they can be applied at home. Some integration of humor is helpful. Within this framework, individuals can learn to laugh at their own shortcomings. Humor diminishes our defenses and heightens our ability to accept help and to work to improve the whole.

Parents must understand the importance of modeling trust if they expect trust in their children. Never was the cliché of "what goes around comes around" more appropriate than in the context of modeling trust with our sons and daughters. Parents need to model trust to friends as well as to family members. Parents need to be clear and concise about their expectations when discussing promises/agreements with their children, and what the consequences are if the promise is broken. They need to provide for compromise without manipulation that may foster mistrust. Helping one's client fully understand and appreciate the value of trust and communication is essential in any therapeutic relationship. It is the mortar that holds the family together. "Troubled young people might leave an adventure course with positive behaviors and good intentions to achieve desirable goals, but these changes, no matter how small, are soon lost in the struggle against poor family interactions and negative community environments" (Durgin and McEwen 1991). Positive family experiences promote better communication, which, in turn, sets a climate in which trust can be built. Helping to direct the family into an activity that they can all enjoy helps to plant the seed that a family can have fun and positive experiences.

Getting through Disdain/Trust and the Tough Guys — A Case Study

John is a 13-year-old boy who came to counseling with nothing to say and a mindset of noncompliance. He was a very angry boy with a difficult past, including sexual abuse and a broken home. He also was experiencing major difficulties at school. He held any and all authority figures in disdain. Initially, no activity was sufficient enough to stimulate his interest. He finally decided to try the climbing wall. John made it two-thirds of the way up and announced he could have made it all the way. "If only I had held the rope tighter." I acknowledged his success in both the log and the wall, as well as his gratitude for my belaying. With a little humor, a pat on the back and accolades for his success, I enthusiastically talked about what we might want to try next time. This was not a time for metaphors or to process the event in-depth. John needed success in a positive challenge, to establish some trust, to feel good, and to experience positive excitement. He needed a place to feel good about and to come back to. Any attempt at verbal therapy would have been an assault on the fun, excitement. and positive experience. There are times when we need to control our ambitions to use our tongue and let the experience alone be the therapy. "Act don't yack," was appropriate in this session, and, in John's case, it wasn't until four more similar sessions before we could begin to discuss other issues. But patience paid off. John had learned to trust and had been successful. Through gradual and continuous reinforcement of such success and the integration of positive growth with school and home, John found some light and hope in his life of anger and despair. This is the first step of the therapeutic process for many.

Family Trust

Trust in the family begins early in the family's relationship and continues throughout life. Parents model trust for their children, which is the most powerful, single, influencing factor in the development of trust among their children. Lack of trust later in childhood and, especially in adolescents is a major contributing factor to the conflicts between parent and child. Trust is so critical to the family structure that without it every other family bond is compromised.

Fun and Family

A family that plays together stays together. Well, perhaps it's not just that easy; however, sharing interest in and enjoying healthy activities together goes a long way toward opening avenues of communication. When family members have some common interests and enjoy those interests together they have something to share (an island of communication). As we continue to develop additional islands of communication we find that conversation flows more freely and communication is open. (Suggestions for recommendations for common activities are listed starting on page 19.)

Sometimes breakthroughs in family communication occur in an activity as simple as bouncing on the trampoline or taking a canoe ride together. The Dawson family of six, for instance, continually bickered. The three younger children, ages 10, 11, and 13, all suffer from Attention Deficit Disorder. Two also suffer from dysthymia. The older daughter, age 16, is doing well, but she is troubled with family responsibilities and continuous crises. Family sessions started well enough, but interruptions became frequent, as each member strived to state his or her case. It became an impulsive free-for-all. Although some of the interruptions were positive in nature, (e.g., request for clarification) others were defensive and some very confrontational. Anger and hostility would gradually build as one would not be able to control his need to defend himself. The family was frequently emotionally dysfunctional and as uptight as a drum. They needed to let loose, have fun, and laugh.

The children were told that if they could take their turn talking, they would all have a turn on the trampoline. The turn-taking incentive was effective. It was more effective to observe the family having fun together and taking turns on the trampoline (timed turns, of course) remarkably well. The family learned through this experience that it could indeed have fun together. The parents also gave it a go, and the family laughed together uncontrollably. As the family returned to the office to close the session, their attitudes, however temporary, were upbeat and much less defensive. Generally, when people feel better about themselves, and share positive time with others, they become much less defensive. When defensiveness is reduced, communication is improved, and the therapeutic process becomes more effective.

We, as therapists, need to fully recognize the value of fun in family therapy. Families need to share and to embrace fun times in order to appreciate time together. A family that doesn't enjoy being together shares a conflict deserving of much attention.

Jim and his mother were constantly at each other, and he was becoming verbally abusive and too difficult to restrain. Jim had witnessed an abusive relationship between his mother and father, who were now divorced. Jim and his mother didn't have much in common and shared little, although Mom tried to connect with her son.

During a family session early one fall evening, with a full moon rising, I suggested that we have our session in a canoe out on the pond. Jim was very receptive and, to his surprise, so was Mom. Jimmy took the stern, Mom was in the bow, and I was granted space in the middle. Being in the stern, Jim was able to select and to control our direction, something that he seldom experienced without criticism. For the first time, I witnessed Jim and his mom listening to each other and even agreeing with each other. Except for Jim's threat that he would tip the canoe over and Mom's response to "go ahead," she was the better swimmer, the session was rewarding for both. Jim needed to be recognized as trusting and capable, and Mom needed Jim to listen to her. We all got our wish, mine being to stay dry.

Some families, having spent part of a session canoeing as a family, will often take it on as a hobby, which also has happened with cross-country skiing, mountain biking, and skating. Families need to experience having fun together, accomplishing family tasks, and trying new activities. As a family develops more similar interests, their level of communication improves. They enjoy being together more often. Parents sometimes need help to realize that the housework will wait, the car will wait, and so will the job, but their children will not wait. Missed family opportunities frequently become a way of life. Counselors, particularly adventure-based counselors, are in the best position to interrupt a cycle of blinded priorities.

9
Adventure-Based Groups

The variety of activities and specific combinations of techniques used in adventure-based group work are as numerous as there are groups. Our focus in this section will be on a number of techniques that we have found to be the most successful and common combinations of techniques.

Group Activities and Assessment

The first step in determining an activity-based direction is to assess the group. The group and its activities may last for hours or for a couple of weeks. It may run continuously or gather on a weekly or monthly basis. Certainly the goals, objectives, and techniques will vary, depending upon the length, size, and needs of the group. To best illustrate the therapeutic design, we will describe several different groups.

At *Adventurelore,* we work with a variety of groups:

- Small group: therapeutic, 2 to 5 participants: 1 1/2 to 3 hours
- Mid-size group: therapeutic, 4 to 8 participants, 1 1/2 to 3 hours
- Adventure trips: 6 to 10 participants: 3 to 6 hours
- School groups: (middle to high school) based on 40 students, 4- to 6-hour program format that focuses on enhancing self-esteem, team-building, and communication skills.
- Large school groups: (at school) 50 to 300 students, 1 1/2- to 3-hour program format.
- Summer outdoor adventure experience: 10 to 15 participants, 6- to 15-day program format.

Although the therapeutic groups will vary significantly, a typical client population will include ADHD youths, ages 12 to 15, who are struggling with social difficulties. Both those who have difficulty in their learning environment and the high achievers tend to develop a greater appreciation for each other's strengths and contributions. A greater sense of working together adds to the growth of all participants. The programs, in general, place primary focus upon enhancing self-esteem, trust, team-building, communication skills, and developing positive social relationships with peers and staff. The accomplishments of these personal objectives pave the way for improved social skills, reduced incidence of depression, greater acceptance and appreciation for others, improvement in the academic environment, and an increased ability to predict, address, and recover from stressful experiences at home and school.

Small Groups — Therapeutic, 2 to 5 participants, 1 1/2 to 3 hours

Nearly all of the participants in these groups are receiving adjunct individual therapy. The group focus is on personal issues, positive development of socially acceptable behaviors, and development of communications and teamwork among peers.

The group generally runs for approximately two hours, every other week. Most of the participants have individual sessions on the alternate week. This schedule allows the counselor and the individual time to process the group experience and to make appropriate behavioral adjustments when necessary and productive. The adventure-based counselor also should provide positive individual activity time during the alternative weeks to enhance self-esteem, trust, and communication skills.

Small-group activities provide an excellent means to help individuals develop socially acceptable behaviors. For the individuals who have difficulty in their social environment, a sufficient amount of individual therapy that focuses on dealing with their more obvious personal issues and social difficulties needs to take place before they join a group. A healthy or improving self-esteem is often critical to that endeavor. It is important that the individual is prepared for the dynamics of a group. Social success is key to changing behaviors. As the individual begins to feel better about himself, he'll portray himself as being more capable and less defensive and will experience greater acceptance from the group. Some children, for instance, have no friends, have experienced few, if any, positive social experiences, and have little success upon which to gauge their behavior. Many of these youths have difficulty with processing their experiences and with impulsiveness. They will benefit initially from positive feedback in the challenges and positive social behaviors through one-to-one counseling. The individual sessions will focus on success, self-confidence, trust, self-esteem, and pragmatic skills. As the individual strengthens his social skills, gradual integration with another child or counselor through a small-group challenge or game will begin. The value here is to establish a positive peer relationship and to reinforce that experience through the success achieved while working or playing together. The initial contacts need to be positive whenever possible. The chain of negative peer relationships must be explored and interrupted through the group process.

94

The next session may provide for a little more interactive time with the chosen peer to set the stage for later positive interaction and shared successes. Although the balance is critical for the most needy individuals, some will mix readily with a peer and, eventually, with small groups. It can be helpful if peers share some common positive interests, (e.g., biking, canoeing, fishing, climbing, etc.) because this helps promote a common and comfortable dialogue. The therapist needs to determine the social status of the individual from parents, school, and early sessions, and then to apply the most appropriate group settings available.

The choice of activities should be noncompetitive, unless the two persons are on the same team. I have found that wrestling-basketball is an excellent tool to use to develop team work and camaraderie, with a very high rating on the fun chart. Wrestling-basketball, like many of the competitive activities, may allow for the two counselors to be on one side and the two clients on the other. This forces a camaraderie in which their success can be controlled and based upon necessary positive reinforcers. The counselors can provide both success and verbal reinforcement to any positive peer (team) interaction. The reinforcers are immediate.

There are several small-group games and activities listed previously in the text. Biking, canoeing, kayaking, fishing, basketball, two-to-two soccer (two staff, two youths), and Moon Ball, are just a few that we have found to be particularly effective during the initial group integration. The length of the activity is based upon what is best for the interactive process for both children, minus three minutes. In other words, end it on a positive note, with both children looking forward to the next group session. During these early sessions with the socially impaired child, it is important to address additional specific needs, to reference medication, and to monitor contact with home and school to assist in the other domains of the child's life. Social growth is improved when islands of success can be provided as reinforcement between sessions. The school may be able to assist in some small-group work by providing the child and the parents insight into a healthy socialization process at home. Most clients do not require the degree of scrutiny in their small groups as does the substantially socially impaired child. Proper matching and proactive counseling are the keys to successful group programming.

Implementing the right activity at the right time is important, and therapeutic spontaneity is essential in order to adjust to the child's needs. Canoeing focuses on group cooperation, while fishing fosters more open dialogue. Mountain biking is good when you suspect that the two individuals might initially need a little more space and a degree of high-intensity activity. The ropes course offers an opportunity to establish greater self-confidence while learning the value of peer support and developing trust as children belay and encourage one another during their challenge. These tend to be higher-level social skills, which makes the ropes course as a group activity more readily used after the children have developed the more basic skills of healthy communication and cooperation. Staff backup on the belay system is generally advised.

Processing at the end of each session encapsulates the experience and allows the individual to review and discuss what went well and to establish new goals. This is a good time to help the child see the connection and the application of the day's experience to his daily life. As to whether we process as a group or individually often depends upon the dynamics of the individuals and the outcome of the session.

The next session may be group or individual. In the early stages of a small adventure-based counseling group, it is often beneficial to alternate weeks, which gives the therapist an opportunity to review and to role play in an individual session the various group situations from both school and counseling experiences. This also leaves time to address other extenuating issues and self-esteem.

As the children progress in their social competence, we can increase the group size by bringing two two-client groups together. This generally is done with two therapists. The processing, whether it is done during or at the end of the session, includes all four clients. These sessions will commonly run for an hour and a half to two hours, which provides for a update on how the week has been going, what focus needs to be applied to the upcoming week, and the choice of group activity. The session will generally close with a group process; however, individual closure can be more beneficial when the counselor needs to re-address issues over and above the group session, or when the counselor feels that bringing up behaviors that would be better talked about in private. Indeed, there are times when the reinforcement through positive recognition of a particular contribution in group may be more meaningful to the child in a private setting.

The goal is to reach the point where the child recognizes his strengths and applies them to his social, home, and academic environments. At the same time, the child needs to recognize his social deficits and work to improve them. The therapist needs to help the child to realize that the gains in his or her social skills are well worth achieving, and to provide a means for bolstering self-esteem. This is achieved best by sharing positive social experiences that are both fun and successful. Contact with school counselors, teachers, and parents is generally helpful in monitoring the level of transference to the real-world environments.

Weekend Multi-Hour, Mid-Size Group Programs, 4 to 8 Participants

Mid-size group programs may have from four to eight clients on weekend adventures. Establishing the proper social climate is important from the onset. Group challenge trips that require travel lend themselves to a social challenge that begins in the van. Prior to departure, it is important for the group to clearly layout the ground rules of peer respect and acceptance. An upbeat predeparture activity effectively breaks down barriers and sets a positive tone for the trip. Right from the get-go, the positive flow of a nonthreatening, friendly, playful atmosphere is established. A key function for staff during the ride is to be proactive and to positively influence the direction of conversation. When this attitude is initiated by a staff member who is respected, has high energy, and is well-liked, it tends to work wonders in setting a positive tone.

Some groups may begin with a session at the home base with a variety of group initiatives and/or a chosen activity, and then spend the latter part of the session planning the next group activity. These groups tend to vary from children and adolescents who are at a high level of social-emotional functioning to those who have significant difficulties in these areas. Because of the length of the trip and the number of kids, the more seriously socially deficient children would generally not attend these groups until they reach a level of social functioning that gives them the resources and the coping skills to have a successful day. To provide a one-to-one counselor-to-client ratio for the more difficult child is often appropriate.

To be successful, these groups generally have a healthy blend of socially positive youths who serve as good models for the struggling youth, and the more socially positive youths, in turn, learn to become more patient and tolerant. These kids often join the group primarily for the adventure itself. The types of success-oriented activities may include mountain biking, rock climbing, ocean canoeing, white-water canoeing, skating, downhill or cross-country skiing. The focus of the day is to have fun while positively interacting, working as a team, and taking on new challenges. The positive energy and intuitiveness of the staff is the major factor of the success of any trip.

The importance of modeling as a powerful counseling tool in this environment should not be overlooked or underestimated. We have had many troubled youths in our program decide that they want to be like one or another of our counselors or college staff. Students who would be expected to drop out of school at age 16 have gone on to college while other troubled youth have found new success in taking up a sport or hobby in which a staff member had participated. It has become well-recognized by many mental-health professionals that a charismatic adult who recognizes and acknowledges the successes and the potential of a particular child or adolescent will have a significant influence on that young person's life. Healthy modeling and recognition of client success is essential.

A Trip to the Marshes

It was a beautiful day in late May, and we were prepared to take a group white-water canoeing. Having had a dry spring and no rain for several days, we realized we'd have to settle for something less than white water. We briefed our group and collectively decided that a tidal river was the next best option. So we headed for the marshes of Rye, New Hampshire.

However small, we encountered a rapid at the put-in spot. As we continued to paddle through the marsh, we came upon a small wooden dam. Because we had been here only during high tide, we had not noticed the dam. On the other side of the dam was mud, with a thin layer of water over it. It had been a beautiful canoe ride up to that point and, although the circumstance was disappointing, we were able to find humor in this surprise. Wanting, of course, to continue, we sent a staff member and two kids down river to see how far we would need to portage before we would reach floatable water.

While we were waiting, the rest of the group played a maneuvering game, in order not to be idle. When our scouts returned, we learned that there was no floatable water within at least a half a mile. So, with a spontaneous burst of energy, Nate, a staff member, took his canoe with his paddling buddy in front and slid it down over the embankment. He landed in the mud up to his ankles and began to push the canoe, which glided over the wet mud. With mud flying from his feet he continued to propel his canoe down the stream. The other kids saw that there was fun to be had in this potentially difficult situation, and that it was okay to get into the mud. They overcame the idea that the mud limited them. Within seconds they all followed, running in and gliding over the mud. Mud races and bumper canoes enhanced the travel. Even after the water became deep enough to paddle, the person in the stern continued to push the canoe. Through this experience, the children learned perseverance by going beyond a negative perception. In processing the day, the children realized that what they had perceived as an inhibitor became an enhancer because they took action (however modeled) in a positive direction. It has been said that life is 10 percent what you're given and 90 percent what you do with it. These kids lived well that day and carried home an experience upon which to build. And we, as staff, had another great day at the "office."

Re-emphasizing Trust

Trust allows groups and co-workers to share ideas for the benefit of the whole. Trust is essential in building relationships. "Faith and trust in self and the other person is such an essential ingredient in relationships that it cuts across and interacts with all other components" (Fitts 1970). Trust allows children to show feelings that were previously hidden, in order to get feedback that can heal years of undisclosed emotional turmoil. Trust allows us to take emotional risks without fear of ridicule, knowing there is an unconditional support. Trust is essential in the cohesive formation of any group. There must be trust in the acceptance of untested ideas.

There is an unlimited resource of trust activities for groups. Many include the use of blindfolds in the Boardwalk, Acid Swamp, and Lead Walk (see Chapter 10). This requires the blindfolded person to be led over a challenge course or series of obstacles while he must rely upon other group members to safely guide him to the end. The processing of such an activity typically focuses upon the idea that we are all blinded in one way or another. In areas about which we know little, we need to trust others. On the other hand, we must respect the power and the responsibility of being trusted.

As an example, on the night hike the group travels a trail on a mountain without using lights. The leader or leaders must feel their way up the trail and communicate any helpful navigating information to the person behind him or her who, in turn, passes it back to the next person. Trust, communication, and patience are essential to the success of the night hike. (The leader should be experienced with the hike and have a flashlight, a first-aid pack, and water.)

The use of the ropes course and rock climbing are both excellent means of developing trust among group members. The Nitro Crossing requires a degree of trust with group members assisting the person swinging over the line. Trust in group consensus and the compass are strengthened through orienteering challenges. "Trust falls" are powerful tools to develop trust in a group. (This should be run only under the supervision of experienced leaders.) Trust in groups and organizations allows the sharing of ideas for the benefit of all invested. (See Chapter 9 on Group Adventure-Based Activities).

Adventure-Based Programming with Large Groups, 40 to 60 Participants

Listed below are a variety of program sizes and formats. These are only examples of some programs. The variations to serve individual populations are endless. With larger groups, of more than 50, we generally begin with a whole-group activity. The goals of such a program typically focus on enhancing communication skills, teamwork, self-confidence, and perseverance. The Lap Sit, (see page 127) is a good activity with which to begin. Because of the nature of this activity, participants should be arranged in the circle so that a tremendous size difference doesn't occur. The arranging and any change in the arrangement needs to be done delicately to prevent any embarrassment. This is a fun, team-building opener that can be repeated at the end of the program.

Another popular activity is the "Aerobic Pump-Up" to music. The music needs to be relatively fast and upbeat. I begin by asking how many participants can ski. Then we practice the movements for skiing. How many can play basketball? Then we practice jumping for a rebound. How many can jump rope? Then we practice jumping rope. After the children have practiced the routines, we incorporate the music and get them moving. You must be enthusiastic. In more than 100 attempts, this activity has only flopped twice. The "flop" provided food for small-group discussions on inhibitions.

After implementing a large-group activity, the large group can be divided into small groups or teams. The teams rotate after each group activity. A typical five-hour program might include a few of the following: The Nitro Crossing, Board Walk, Cheese Please, Spider Web, All Aboard, Human Knot, Swamp Walk, Blind Man's Pass, Acid Swamp, Flash Flood, and a variety of low-ropes course group challenges (See Chapter 10). Each activity would be scheduled and designed to take approximately 25 minutes and to allow three to five minutes more for processing the activity in greater depth. Collective processing of all the activity generally takes place at the end of the morning program. The groups commonly finish their morning challenges with a team-orienteering competition. Each group will be given an orienteering course to complete. The afternoon program offers the participants an opportunity to challenge themselves and/or to encourage others on the ropes course, mountain bikes and/or to become involved in waterfront activities, such as canoeing, kayaking, and sailing. The afternoon program, as stated, applies to programs run at the adventure-based facility.

Ideally, we like to include time at the end of the program for each group to perform a skit on the focus of the day. The skits have not only been entertaining but informative, reinforcing, and the opportunity for some "lesser stars" to shine.

The debriefing includes congratulations to all for making it through "alive," emphasizing specific points of helping one another, cooperative efforts, surprising and gutsy accomplishments, and reinforcing the importance of the follow-through into their lives. In school settings, teachers often will incorporate the theme of the program into their curriculum to reinforce the theme and the effect of the day.

Middle School Activity-Based Programs

The focus in this section will be upon the development of self-esteem, self-confidence, team-building, and positive group integration among middle-school students. The student population will be approximately equal in male and females. As always, students will be greeted by the adventure staff. We generally try to maintain a ratio of one counselor to eight or 10 students in these groups. The entire group of students will gather in a circle to receive a warm and enthusiastic greeting and then be asked questions randomly, to stimulate immediate input. By establishing an early two-way rapport, the students feel freer to act. An enthusiastic, semi-humorous, preview of the morning's activities will be given. We encourage the interjection of some humor to keep the atmosphere upbeat. The emphasis on teamwork and the point that each person has some strength and something to offer is made clear. When most participants feel welcome, comfortable, and ready to go, our first objective has been accomplished.

The first activity may be the "Lap Sit," "Sinking Ships," or the "Human Knot." As described in the group-activities section, The "Human Knot" helps to break down inhibition, stimulate communication, and creates an ethic about working together. The "Lap Sit," and "Sinking Ships" provides a community challenge that leads to team cooperation and fosters team success — success by the group, for the group. For groups that will be together for more than half-day or that are smaller in size, a "name game" is usually beneficial. The above format is a good opening for any size and length of group. Remember, the opening of any program profoundly influences the total effect of the program.

Large-Group Program

Program for 100 students at their school, outdoors, 4 1/2 hours

Objective: to enhance communication skills, team-building, and a sensitivity to the needs of others. Self-confidence and self-esteem also will be addressed through the emphasis on healthy behavioral patterns.

Agenda:

- group opening/hearty introduction
- giant Lap Sit/Sinking Ships
- aerobic pump-up
- directions for the day

Teachers may have already divided students into groups, which sometimes provides for the most effective results. Twenty-five minutes plus three minutes for processing the activity is allotted for each challenge station. Two minutes should be allotted for the transition from one activity to another. We allot 30 minutes for the opening, two and one-half hours for the activities, a 30-minute lunch, and 30 minutes in which groups prepare skits that depict their impressions of the day. We divide 30 minutes among the groups for each group to present their skits. The final 30 minutes is used for recognition and to process the day.

Mid-Size Group Program

Program for 40 students at Adventurelore Base Camp; 6 1/2 hours

Objective: to build self-confidence, communication skills, team-building, sensitivity toward others, and self-esteem.

Agenda:

- Opening (welcome, introductions, statement of the day's purpose)
- Ice-breaker activity in a circle to become better acquainted (staff, faculty are included)
- Directions for the morning schedule
- Large-group challenge activity
- Initiation of small-group activities (four groups rotate among four activities)
- Orienteering challenge (remain in small groups for the challenge)
- Lunch and group processing of the morning
- Afternoon activities
- Processing the experiences of the day

Note: Programs work best when the day goes from more-structured to less-structured activities.

Winter Program

Program for 40 students at *Adventurelore* Base Camp

Objective: to develop a healthy attitude about the appreciation for the outdoors during the winter, to develop a greater understanding of winter safety, to build self-confidence and group-cooperation skills

Agenda:

- Opening (30 minutes)
  - » Welcome
  - » Introduction of staff
  - » Opening dialogue
  - » Preview of the day's activities and their objectives
- Large-group activity (20 to 30 minutes)
- Small-group activities
  - » Group A - Winter survival/interactive seminar
  - » Group B - Skating
  - » Group C - Cross-country skiing
  - » Group D - Ropes course

(These groups rotate every hour, with a 10-minute cocoa break after the second hour.)

- The entire group comes together in the original groups and spends approximately one hour on the orienteering-challenge course.
- Lunch break after orienteering activity or a third group activity
- Free choice of activity (one hour)
  (Can include any of the above activities or the trampoline, and/or wrestling-basketball.)
- Processing the experience of the day and closing.

Note: Programs of this nature work best when the activities are presented in a sequence of more-structured to less-structured.

Extra-Large Group — Off Site

Program for up to 300 students, at their school; three hours in the morning.

Objective: to enhance positive behavioral patterns, self-esteem, communication, and group skills.

Agenda:

- Opening (40 minutes - interactive presentation)
- To save time, the students are arranged into several small groups by teachers or staff prior to the start of the program. The challenge activity may consist of several small-group challenges or, more commonly, one large-group challenge. (Activities can include: Multi-dimensional Board Walk in which groups would have access to different items with which to reach a particular goal as a team; hoop pass; giant All Aboard; team-rescue challenge/Sinking Ships)
- Closing, with group processing

Note: The groups for this program will have been prearranged in teams of 20.

Groups of 16 to 24 Participants

Program lasts for 5 hours, at Base Camp

Objective: to develop appreciation and acceptance of others, to build self-esteem, self-confidence, teamwork, and communication skills, to have fun in a healthy environment, and to learn to persevere through a difficult challenge.

Agenda:

- Opening (30 minutes)
  (Includes welcome, introductions, whole-group activity, review of activities to come and division into groups of six to eight participants)

- Groups participate in separate activities. One group goes mountain biking, the other takes on the ropes course. At the end of an hour, they exchange activities.

- Lunch (30 minutes)

- Group activities
  One group does orienteering, the other does canoeing/sailing. At the end of one hour, the groups exchange activities.

- Process the events of the day

A Note on Competition

In the past, adventure-based practitioners have been divided as to whether competition detracts from or enhances an adventure-based program. After thousands of observations, it is our impression that some healthy competition makes the program more exciting and beneficial to the participants. The effect certainly could vary from group to group. A simple survey of the group will often help the group leaders make the choice. There are, however, components of the program, (e.g., the ropes course, orienteering, rock climbing, collectively covering a certain distance in one day, etc.) in which universal support, not competition, is far more important.

Competition can be employed by the whole group to accomplish a particular goal, perhaps in a certain amount of time, or in a timed-and-scored competition with another team within that same program. Three factors play a role in the competitive format: the size of the group, the general make-up of the group, and the group's objectives. Group sizes of 12 or fewer people often lend themselves best to one team working together, setting it's own goals, and trying to achieve them. It is sometimes better when the staff assesses the group and assist in establishing realistic goals for them. An experienced practitioner can help promote a positive climate. It is important for staff persons to remember that groups are here to learn and to develop self-esteem and camaraderie. Adventure-based practitioners are, in essence, teachers and counselors in a very subtle way. We often need to set the atmosphere and to enhance the dynamics of the group in order to help them to realize their maximum potential. The positive experience itself will then result in learning. Nothing teaches as well as experience.

10
Challenge Activities*

In this chapter, we offer the specifics of our various challenge activities. Some of the activities are problem-solving initiatives where there is no single right or wrong answer. The path taken along the way to the solution is most important.

Although the level of physical activity varies from game to game, each game is cooperative in nature. Cooperative activities provide the opportunity and encouragement for individuals to participate at his or her own physical and emotional level with improved communication, self-esteem, and team-building components being the primary benefits of play.

The degree of competitiveness of some cooperative games can be adjusted to fit the needs of the group. An experienced facilitator can make the necessary adjustments with minimal interference and significantly improve the value of the activity for the group. Don't be afraid to be creative and custom design certain activities to best serve particular group needs.

The variety of activities presented here will provide you with a repertoire of group challenges that can be employed in small or large spaces. Some of the games may require a "spotter" or a staff person who assists with the safety or supporting of the more difficult components of the game. Safety should be the number one concern. For further assistance in spotting, we recommend you refer to the list of suggested readings and/or attend adventure-based seminars such as Project Adventure, Adventurelore, or NOLS. We caution you not to economize on the use of "spotters" as they are necessary for safe programming. To assist you in this area, a safety tip is included as a criterion for each game. You may also wish to seek out a physical education specialist in your school or at the local college to provide teaching tips for the more difficult activities and to help you with spotting techniques.

*Developed with Eileen Sullivan, Ed.D., Boston University.

The 14 games are listed in alphabetical order and described in the same format with: Benefits, Playing Area, Equipment, Game Objectives, Rules of Play, Modifications, Safety Issues, and Processing. Processing, often at intervals during and at the end of each activity, is a form of debriefing with the participants. The facilitator leads a discussion of what happened during the activity to strengthen team communication. Participants should be encouraged to talk about the process, how the problem was solved or how the team played in a game situation. There should not be finger pointing and individuals should be encouraged to form opinions in positive statements or constructive criticism directed toward the team or group. "Perhaps we needed to communicate better, " or "We did not listen to everyone," are the types of statements the facilitator is seeking during processing. Avoid, "Suzy didn't do anything to help," or "Bobby wouldn't try my idea." Instead, direct the group towards analyzing their abilities to work together, come together to solve a given problem, and be accepting of all individuals. In a more therapeutic setting, we need to listen to the accusatory statements, recognize their origin, and help the whole group address such issues and model the appropriate method of addressing those issues. The diagram and/or picture at the end of each description shows player and game organization.

All Aboard

Easiest Level

This activity originated at the Hurricane Island Outward Bound and was brought to *Adventurelore* by Tom Andrews.

☑ Benefits: To break down inhibitions and touch barriers, to foster group cohesiveness, to learn to work together as a team to solve a problem, to enhance communication among teammates.

✎ Equipment: One small square platform of a sturdy material raised a few inches off the ground. (A two-foot by two-foot square can hold from 12 to 15 adults; a one foot by one foot can hold eight players.) Larger squares could accommodate different size groups or use fewer people in groups to not draw special attention to the physical attributes of a group without embarrassment.

⬚ Playing Area: Inside or outside; minimum space requirement.

🚶 Players: Eight to 15 per group. (The larger the group the more difficult the activity.)

▦ Game Objectives: To get the entire group onto the platform for a specified amount of time. Try requiring five seconds for the first attempt, and then play it again and require eight to 10 seconds.

▤ How to Play: The players in a group work together by talking and then arranging themselves onto the raised platform so all their body parts are off the ground. Players are free to use any method of getting all the players onto the platform as long as the method meets with the group's approval.

⇧ Modifications: Vary the size of the group or the speed count to heighten the effect and suspense. If a variable speed count is employed, make sure it has a positive effect on the group. There should be success for all the participants with this activity. This activity can also be played on the floor with different size hula hoops if a raised platform is not available.

Safety Issues: Review spotting techniques and remind the group they must tell the facilitator how they will solve the problem. If a pyramid is suggested, the facilitator will have to intervene and review safety procedures and provide spotters. Be aware of weight distribution with adults and children.

Processing: Ask how the group worked together? Was everyone's opinion respected? Did they consider the uniqueness of each individual? How could they solve the problem more efficiently next time?

All Aboard

Blind Man's Pass

Intermediate/Advanced Level

This activity originated at *Adventurelore* in 1997.

Benefits: To teach communication skills, teamwork, the ability to focus, and to enhance eye-hand coordination skills.

Equipment: Twelve tennis balls, eight Hoola Hoops (or rings of similar size), three blindfolds, one large basket or large trash can.

Playing Area: Large field or gymnasium with the eight hoops/rings arranged as in the diagram.

Players: Nine players per team; one starter, three "blind" passers chosen to wear blindfolds, three sighted catchers, a chaser, and a shooter.

Game Objectives: Version 1: For each team to get as many balls in the basket within a specified amount of time (12 minutes). Version 2: For each team to get all 12 balls in the basket in the least amount of time.

How to Play: The starter, the passers, and the catchers must keep at least one foot in the hoop at all times. The starter at hoop #1 throws a ball to the catcher at hoop #2. The catcher hands the ball to the blind" passer in hoop #2. Then the blind passer takes verbal directions from the catcher to pass the ball to the catcher at hoop #3. The play continues in this format. The chaser collects any balls that miss the catcher by returning them to the starter. The starter then restarts that ball. If the chaser chooses to throw the ball to the starter, rather than delivering it, and the starter misses the ball, the chaser must retrieve the ball for the starter. Play continues until all the balls are in the bucket or the time has expired.

Modifications: Number of players can vary by adding more hoops to accommodate other "blind" passers or sighted catchers. Additional starters and chasers or two rows of play per team could be arranged. Greater distance between the hoops would increase the level of difficulty of play while a shorter distance between the hoops would create an easier level of play.

⊕ Safety Issues: Younger players should be reminded to use good communication to pass the ball. Use a question format to challenge and to probe how to best pass the balls. A lead- up activity of passing to the "blind" passers could be played to reinforce communication. Stress communication, listening to partners, and efficiency rather than speed. Sorry, that was my editor talking, speed adds to the fun and excitement.

Processing: It may be necessary to intervene throughout the play to encourage teamwork. Pose questions like: How can you communicate better? What "cues" do you need to provide to the unsighted players? Talk about communication as well as the abilities to listen, focus, direct, throw, catch and run. How do verbal and nonverbal commands come into play?

Note: The number of participants can vary, as can the number of balls and length of time. We find that the aforementioned presentation is most commonly ideal for our groups. The distance also can be adjusted, depending upon the capability and developmental stage of the group. Another option is to rotate players from one position to another (except passers).

Processing: Communications *v.* confusion — handling frustration so it doesn't impair one's ability to perform. Using various strengths, such as ability to listen, focus, direct, catch, throw, run, etc.

Blind Man's Pass

Blind Man's Pass

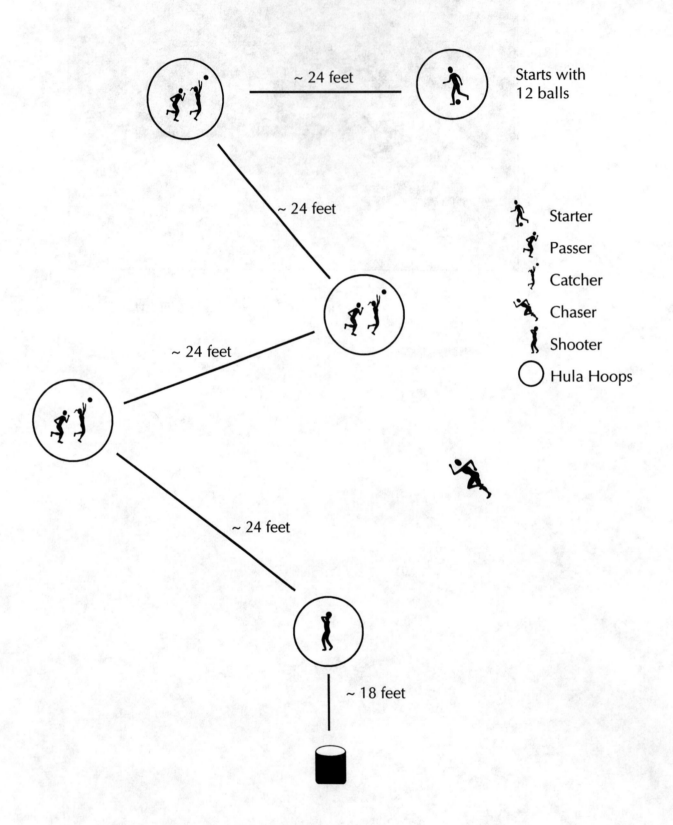

~ 24 feet

Starts with
12 balls

~ 24 feet

Starter

Passer

Catcher

Chaser

Shooter

Hula Hoops

~ 24 feet

~ 24 feet

~ 18 feet

The Board Walk

Easy to Intermediate Level of Difficulty

This activity was developed at *Adventurelore* in 1984 and continues to be a favorite. A similar activity originated at Outward Bound in North Carolina in the late 1960's.

✓	**Benefits:**	To improve communication skills and teamwork through a group problem-solving activity.
	Equipment:	Boards that are two inches thick and one foot square. One or two fewer boards per player are needed. (A team of six could play the game with four or five boards, depending upon ages and playing area.)
	Playing Area:	Best played outside in an open area or large field but can be modified to a smaller scale in a gymnasium. Ideal area is at least 30 yards by 20 yards for six teams of eight to 10 participants. The number of participants in each team determines the size of the playing area.
	Players:	Groups from three or four to 20. Adjust the number of players in the group to suit the size of the playing area, the age of the players and the size of the entire group.
	Game Objectives:	To solve the problem of moving all the players on a team across an "electrified" playing field from the starting line to the finish line (Point A to Point B on the diagram, which is usually 25 yards or more yards apart.)
	How to Play:	The facilitator explains to the players that they must move everyone across an "electrified" field, and the means is "The Board Walk," or the use of the boards which are "safe zones." The players are provided the boards (usually one or two less than the number of players in the group), and they are free to use them in any way they like to get home. Players are safe on the boards but if a body part touches the ground, or the "electrified" field, he or she is "jolted" back to the start. The teams are given 60 seconds to huddle and make a plan to get the whole team across the "electrified" field. The amount of time alloted to complete the task is variable or unlimited. Any number of players can

be on one board at a time. If played inside, the boards cannot be slid across the floor but must be picked up. Often a half-way point is used to move the play along. If a team has passed the half-way point and a player steps off a board, that player begins again at the half way point instead of at the starting line.

 Modifications: For fewer than four players, use one board per player. In groups of seven to 12, one board fewer than the number of players is recommended. For groups of 12 to 20, two boards fewer than the number of participants is recommended. The number of boards and the size of the playing field determines the level of difficulty of play. Vary one or both of these factors to increase or decrease complexity for players. Blindfold one or two players to increase the level of difficulty of play and enhance the nurturing element of the game. Often groups will want to play again. Time could be introduced as a factor if the group is interested. Use processing time before playing for a second time and ask the group how they could work together in a more efficient way? What will they do differently the second time? Why?

 Safety Issues: Facilitators should step back but be aware of how each team is placing the boards on the ground or floor and intervene if necessary. Boards used on tile or wood floors may slip as participants leap onto them.

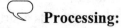 **Processing:** Encourage discussion about how the group worked together to solve the problem. Was there one leader or did everyone contribute? Initiate support about how the group finalized their movement pattern across "The Board Walk," and whether all opinions were respected.

Board Walk

Capture the Flag

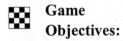

Benefits: An active game that energizes both youth and adult groups, fosters insight, enhances teamwork, and requires communication. Individuals play at their own levels and physical speed and agility are advantageous but often a "smart" team without the physical skills prevails in the end.

Equipment: Two flags, scarves, bean bags, or items to snatch or capture. The flags could be commercial school flags, towels, sweatshirts, or our favorite — life jackets. Rope or cones can be used to mark the boundary line between the teams and the end lines. Team pinnies or shirts to distinguish teams can also be used.

Playing Area: Large playing area, preferably outside.

Players: Each team consists of an equal number of players with a minimum of six to eight on a team, but the game is best played with large teams of 10 to 14 or 16 per team. One player from each team is designed as a flag guard and a second player becomes the jailer.

Game Objectives: To capture the other team's flag on their teammate's side of play.

How to Play: Teams are created, and each team positions itself on its own half of the playing field. Facilitators should allow a few minutes for teams to discuss strategies of play. There are few rules here. Each team member is safe on their own half of the field, but when they venture into their teammate's half, where they must go to get the flag, they may be tagged. If tagged in their teammate's half of the field, they are sent to jail. To get out of jail, the imprisoned player must be tagged by one of his teammates while he is making contact with the prison, be it a tree, post, rock, or cone. The players may make a human chain to extend their reach and to make a get-free tag from a teammate easier. The human chain must be fully connected to the jail in order for the prisoners to be freed. Each team selects a flag guard and a jailer. The flag guard stands at least 15 feet (about five steps) from the flag they are guarding on their own half of the field. The flag guard protects the flag and is free to tag an opponent who tries to capture the flag. A jailer from each team can stand as close to the jail as he or she chooses.

Modifications: Use different means of getting out of jail. For example, in some games if the prisoner or prisoners tag the jailer while making contact with the jail, they all become free, but must get back over the center line without being tagged to be safe. In most games, if a player from Team A grabs Team B's flag and runs off with it but gets caught before crossing the center line, they, of course, go to jail and the flag stops at the point at which the player from Team A was caught. A variation to that method is to return the flag to its original spot.

Safety Issues: Not many concerns here other than safe tagging and the use of a safe playing area without holes in the ground.

Processing: An honor code should be encouraged here. If a player tags an opponent, there should not be name calling but rather honesty in play. Be sure to provide time for teams to talk about their strategies of play. How can the teams use offensive and defensive tactics for better play? How can each individual use his or her physical or mental strengths to achieve the common goal of capturing the flag? Communication is key, and the participants should be questioned about how they can work together for more efficient play.

Capture the Flag

Capture the Flag

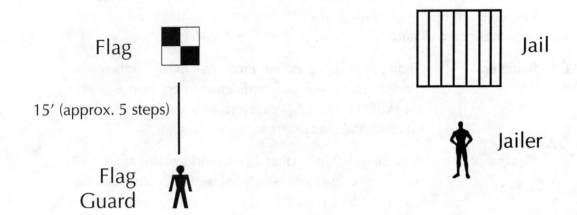

Flag

15' (approx. 5 steps)

Flag
Guard

Jail

Jailer

Mid-Boundary Line — Red Team

- -

Mid-Boundary Line — Blue Team

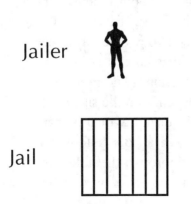

Jailer

Jail

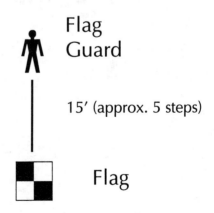

Flag
Guard

15' (approx. 5 steps)

Flag

Cheese Please/ Spider Web

We were introduced to Spider Web by friends who used it at Project Adventure and the originator was John Jarboe from Pennsylvania. Cheese Please, a modification of Spider Web, invented by *Adventurelore* in 1995, is a similar game but the equipment is easier to transport and store.

Benefits:
Emphasizes cooperative problem-solving techniques. Stresses individual self-confidence to perform a physical skill. To learn how to work in a group and respect opinions and trust others to achieve a goal.

Equipment:
A piece of yellow material (felt works well), at least 10 feet by five feet, into which holes of different sizes are cut. The holes must be large enough for a player to be passed through the holes of the "cheese" without touching the sides.

Playing Area:
The "cheese" should be hung between two trees or between two posts that are securely anchored in the ground. The bottom of the cheese should touch the ground. The height of the cheese is determined by the group dynamics. A few inches above the knees of the participants is generally a good height. This activity could be played inside or outside, a soft surface is preferred. A tumbling mat could be used inside.

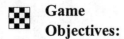 **Players:**
For the "cheese" size here, a small group of six to eight or 10 works best.

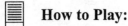 **Game Objectives:**
To move each member of the team through the holes of the "cheese" without touching the sides.

How to Play:
Players take time to reflect on how to them to move each individual through the holes without touching the sides. Players must not touch the sides. If they do, that individual must start again. Once two people have been passed through the same hole, that hole is considered "closed" and may not be used again. (The number of people it takes to close a hole depends on the size of the group. With a larger group of 12 or more, then perhaps three people have to pass through a hole before it is closed.) When people are passed through the hole, they can and should still be active in the game by assisting

with spotting or support. The team should establish a team strategy to ensure that there are enough players to lift, push, and support the larger and less-able players, and the players who are better suited for different size holes. The challenge is complete when all the players have successfully been passed through the "cheese" holes without touching a side.

Modifications: Play once with a moderately low height for the "cheese" then increase the level of difficulty by raising the height. After processing, a time element could be added as a challenge. (A group of 10 to 12 players should be able to move through the "cheese" in 15 minutes. Scoring could be introduced for a competitive spirit. A point is scored each time a player touches the side of the "cheese." A team point is deducted each time a player successfully passes through a hole without touching the side. The team with the lower score completes the challenge more successfully.

Safety Issues: Spotters are a requirement for this challenge. Each team may select several spotters to stand on the receiving side of the cheese as players pass through the holes. We as a staff generally backup the spotters. The team elects how and when to have the participants move through the holes, but safety must be the main concern. The facilitator may need to review spotting techniques and weight distribution with the team members.

Processing: Encourage the group to "think through" the problem before rushing into the active process. Question the group as to how they decided on a means of moving people through the cheese. Was there a specific strategy? Why? How were individual strengths utilized? Did each player trust his teammates? Why or why not? Was each individual's opinion respected and heard before one solution was used? Discuss how the group could improve their communication skills to solve the challenge faster and safer a second time around.

Passing through the cheese

Duck Game/Towel Tag

We believe the Duck Game originated from Outward Bound in the 1970's. However, Chris Troy first brought it to us in 1995.

Benefits: Emphasizes teamwork, communication, problem-solving skills, stimulates creativity, joy of activity, and teaches adults and children how to play through physical activity.

Equipment: At least two tightly rolled and taped towels; duct tape works well here, and a pattern could be created with colored tape.

Playing Area: Sixty foot circle for 20 players or an open area with boundaries.

Players: Game accommodates 10 to 100 players; just add more towels, make the circle larger or form smaller groups in smaller circles.

Game Objectives: To tag everyone in the group with a towel.

How to Play: In a game with 20 players, start with two or three people with a wrapped towel. There are the "its" who pursue other players by tossing the towels to each other or to themselves. The "its" cannot move with the towel in their possession, but rather must figure out how to tag others without running or walking with the towel. These "its" could toss the towel in the air, run, catch the towel to tap someone, or pass the towels to each other in order to catch up to a not-it player. Tossing towels in the air to oneself and then running ahead is allowed, too. The players who become tagged by the "its" become "its" and thus involved in the towel tagging process. A player, "it," must have possession of the towel when tapping a not-it player. Therefore, a not-it hit by a thrown towel is still not-it. This is an active game with few rules but once it is played, the players young and old will want to play again.

Modifications: Instead of playing until everyone in the group is tagged, try using a time element. Set an appropriate time and see how well the group works together and how many players can be tagged in a set time. Play, process, and then try again.

Safety Issues: Review tagging procedures and boundaries. Head tags are not allowed. When the area is inside or the playing area is smaller than suggested, a walk only rule for all players may be implemented.

Processing: Talk about the joy of the activity after playing, the value of teamwork, and how important communication figured into the success of the game. How could communication be improved? How could the group use verbal and nonverbal cues to tag people faster? **Note:** Be sure not to provide too much detailed information on how to tag others in this game. The process is as significant as the result. The players need to figure out how to tag others themselves.

Duck Tag for 60 people requires vigilence and teamwork

Human Knot/The Tangle

We believe this game originated with the Appalachian Mountain Club out of Boston, Massachusetts. Karl Rohnke has modified the activity by using panty hose as an extension of each hand. Karl recommended the panty hose idea to us. The suggested box of 200 panty hose delivered last week to the office has prompted many a question. *Adventurelore* was introduced to the game by Tom Andrews, M.Ed., the builder of our ropes course in 1984.)

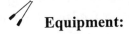 **Benefits:** Improves group communication through the sharing of ideas, reduces the inhibition to close contact with people and promotes fun and a challenge to solve a problem.

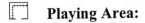 **Equipment:** None, however, panty hose could be used as an extension from each hand with the activity.

Playing Area: No special requirements. Open space large enough for the group size to stand in a circle.

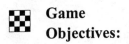 **Players:** The activity works best with eight to 12 players per group. The smaller the group size, the greater the chance for assured success. One option is to start with small groups of six or eight then combine two groups for double the size.

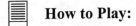 **Game Objectives:** To create a tangle free circle or a figure eight without breaking hand-to-hand connections with the players. (If the players grasp hands correctly, the solution will always be a circle or a figure eight.)

How to Play: Have the players stand in a relaxed circle. Ask them to step forward until the shoulders of each player are touching each other. Each player reaches forward, first with the left hand to grasp someone else's left hand or wrist, and then with the right hand to grasp another person's right hand or wrist. In order for a solution, be sure to see that players do not grasp both hands, right and left, of the same player. (Trick: tell the players right hand above and grab a wrist, then left hand down low and take another hand or wrist. It is easier to "see" the connection here.) Now, without unclasping hands or breaking the connections, the group tries to untangle themselves to create a tangle free circle or figure eight.

 **Modifications:** Add some positive humor to help reduce the natural barriers that occur during this type of "close" physical contact activity. Take into consideration the age and capabilities of the group when determining circle sizes. It is better to begin with smaller circles than too large as the group may become overly frustrated.

Safety Issues: Remind the players to be considerate of each other's hand holding and talk about the moves before doing them.

Processing: Talk about how players felt with the "closeness" of the activity, how communication helped, and whether the group had fun. Was there one leader or did everyone work well together? Did everyone feel that their input was listened to? How could the group solve the problem more efficiently the next time?

Human Knot

Lap Sit

Benefits: Demonstrates the need for the group to work together, helps reduce the inhibition of close contact, and provides a fun means of prompting cohesion.

Equipment: No equipment needed.

Playing Area: Large enough area to accommodate the group in a circle.

Players: All the players have the same role in the game. No special designations.

Game Objectives: To form a circle with each player sitting on the knees of the player behind him or her.

How to Play: Players stand shoulder to shoulder in a tight circle. On the count of three, all players turn clockwise one-quarter turn. After turning clockwise, the players take two or three steps sideways toward the center, staying directly behind the player in front of him or her. Facilitators should assist with the alignment of the players according to size and abilities. For example, heavier people should support each other, or be together in the circle. This arrangement should be performed discretely in order to avoid issues with weight, feelings, and embarrassment. When the players are aligned, tell them to bend their knees slightly (about 30 degrees) on the count of one. On the count of two, the players should bend their knees to a 60 degree angle, and on a count of three, they attempt to actually sit on the knees of the player behind them.

Modifications: Try this activity in a line format or other shapes. Ask the group to say their alphabet or to take some steps together when they are sitting on each other's knees, "right" and "left" usually ends up with everyone laughing and falling on the floor.

Safety Issues: As discussed in the rules of play, be sure to be aware of weight issues and special considerations. Take care when working with a group of older adults or players who have physical issues or back problems. A soft surface or mat would be best to have underneath special populations.

Processing: What effect does one player have on another and to the success of the group? Talk about how comfortable the players felt trusting the person in front of them and behind them. Try doing this activity at the beginning and at the end of a session. The double effort will usually result in a significant improvement in the group's cohesiveness.

Lava Acid Swamp

This activity originated at Outward Bound in the late 1960's and was brought to *Adventurelore* by a friend. We have altered the activity to increase the level of excitement. It's always challenging and usually fun.

Benefits: Promotes group cooperation and the use of individual skills. Requires some analytical thinking and application. Fosters listening and communicating with others as well as expressing one's opinions and ideas to a group. Each player's strength, balance, and consideration of others is used to solve an active problem.

Equipment: Three "four-by-four" beams, eight feet long. (Three sets of "two-by-four" boards bolted together make a stronger piece of equipment.) Twelve stumps about 12 inches in diameter and four to eight inches high. **Note:** cinder blocks or 12-inch square boards that are one inch thick, may be substituted. Three squares nailed together makes a three-inch-high platform for better height.

Playing Area: A large, wide-open playing area is required. Could be modified to be played inside a large space or gymnasium.

Players: Eight to 12 participants per Swamp is a functional size group.

Game Objectives: To move the group safely across the "Acid Swamp" by figuring out how to connect the stumps with the beams provided.

How to Play: The distances of the 12 stumps are arranged so that the beams cannot be connected diagonally. Players are in a group at the starting line and must figure out a way to use the equipment to cross the Lava Acid Swamp without touching the ground. The ground has "lava acid" and if a player falls into the swamp or any body part touches the acid, then that player must return to the start. Each beam has three "lives" and each time a beam touches the swamp it loses a "life." The loss of the lives of each beam should be recorded by the staff or a facilitator. When a beam loses it's three lives, then that beam is removed from play. The team members must develop a strategy for placing the beams between the stumps in order to get the team across the swamp. Should everyone cross together? What is the best strategy? Remember, if there are four people on a beam, and they fall into the swamp, all four players start again. Should the team risk a beam in a critical situation if it only has one life left?

Modifications: Use a time limit for an older age group or a group that can handle challenge. A scoring system could be employed. One point for each player who makes it safely across the swamp. One point is deducted for each fall into the swamp. One point is deducted each time a beam touches the acid after its three "lives." Use scoring to challenge groups to better their ability to solve the problem. Use more tiers of stumps to make the problem more difficult. Challenge a group which has successfully completed the problem by eliminating one or two stumps to increase the level of difficulty. The goal is to foster team success, so it is necessary to be flexible when setting up and working with this activity.

Safety Issues: Reinforce how to work with the boards and place them so fingers are not underneath the beams. Stress communication to the group.

Processing: The processing is as important as the activity. Be sure to allow the time to process this activity at the end of play and before playing again. Elicit responses from each player without finger pointing or even using names. Have the group say, "We needed to," or "The group should have," instead of using individual names. Did anyone feel they were shunned or their opinion was ignored? Why? How did teamwork enhance the effort of and ultimately the success or failure of the group. Do you feel more or less ready to share your insights and opinions with your group? How could the group improve their communication skills to solve the problem? **Note:** The Board Walk is a good lead-up activity to this problem.

Lava Acid Swamp

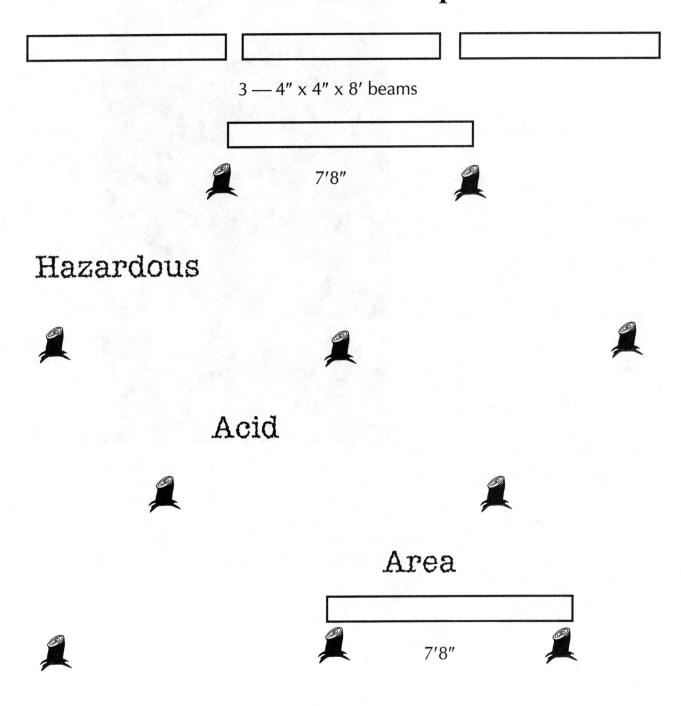

3 — 4″ x 4″ x 8′ beams

7′8″

Hazardous

Acid

Area

7′8″

- - - - - - - - - - - SAFETY LAND - - - - - - - - - - - -

131

Lava Acid Swamp

Mohawk Walk

The Mohawk Walk was first built, used, and named at Triton Regional High School during a Pennsylvania workshop in the early 1980's. Two Mohawk Indians in the workshop group asked to have the activity named after their tribe in Montreal, Canada.

Benefits: Teamwork, strategy skills, balance, trust, and cooperation.

Equipment: A Mohawk Walk is constructed by connecting a wire or rope, strung about eighteen inches above the ground, to the base of two trees. For construction of low-ropes course elements, refer to suggested readings in the ropes-course manual. The length of the wire will be determined by the space between the trees. Longer wire length designates a longer and more difficult activity. If possible, design the course in such a way that it becomes progressively more difficult for the participants to move across the wires for the walk.

Playing Area: This is a stationary low-ropes course element.

Players: Four to 12 participants is a recommended size.

Game Objectives: To move each member of a group across a series of wires or ropes strung from tree to tree. Participants attempt to walk the wires between the trees using only themselves, each other, and the trees for support.

How to Play: We use a four-section Mohawk Walk that gets progressively more difficult. The team points are awarded as each section is completed by a participant. One point per tree is awarded per participant. For example, if four participants make it to tree two and three participants make it to tree three, the team would gain eight points (two points each) for the first four participants because the made it from tree one (1 point) to tree two (1 point) and nine additional points for three participants making it to tree three. The participants are awarded points based upon where they end up at the end of a given time to complete the challenge, typically 12 minutes. If a participant touches the ground, he or she has to return to

133

the beginning. Participants may not use any foreign objects (sticks, ropes, etc.) to keep them on the wire.

Modifications: The group may elect to use a human tree, which can be placed in any one spot along the walk. Once the human tree has been touched by a Mohawk Walker, the tree can no longer move his trunk (feet), however, his limbs (arms) can sway in any way to help the walkers. For less capable groups, more human trees can be placed along the walk. Staff need to place themselves most appropriately in order to spot the participants. The position and the number of spotters depends upon the course.

Processing: The decision whether to use the human tree and how the groups arrived at that decision should be processed. Generally, some or most of the participants will try to cross the wire by themselves and fail. Process what prompted them to try another method; perhaps using the whole group. Issues of listening, trust, and sacrificing for the good of the group are all issues that the processing of the Mohawk Walk lends itself to.

Mohawk Walk

134

Moon Ball *Adventurelore* Style

Credit must be given to Karl Rohnke's book, *Quicksilver,* Steve Butler, and Project Adventure. Our *Adventurelore* modifications differ, but adapt and invent your own versions of the game.

☑ **Benefits:** Develops cooperation, quick teamwork passing skills, and a fun activity for any age group as an "ice-breaker" activity or a problem solving game. Communication among team players is stressed and necessary in order to succeed.

✏ **Equipment:** A beachball, or two beach balls if two teams play against each other.

▢ **Playing Area:** An open field or large playing area.

👫 **Players:** Any size group. If working with large numbers, have several teams.

▨ **Game Objectives:** To move a beachball the entire length of a field in the shortest amount of time, or, if playing against another team, to move a beachball to the other end of the field before the opponent does.

▤ **How to Play:** Players spread out in any fashion and the ball is put into play by one player on the starting line. The person that hit the ball into the air cannot touch the ball again until each member of the team has had a turn to hit it. By using all parts of the body, the players attempt to keep the ball in the air and at the same time move it to the other end of the field. If the ball touches the ground or if a player hits the ball before everyone on the team has touched it, play begins back at the starting line. If two teams are playing against each other, play could begin on the center line or each team could begin at opposite ends of the field with two separate balls.

☑ **Modifications:** Change the format of play, the time, and the group, depending on how long it takes to accomplish the goal of moving the beachball to the opposite end of the field. Modify the boundaries and make the game easier by decreasing the size of the playing field. Increase the level of difficulty by adding a second ball for the group to

135

keep up in the air, or by requiring a boy-girl pattern. Try Karl Rohnke's version of the game and ask the group to keep track of the number of hits they use to keep the beachball up in the air.

Safety Issues: Make sure players spread out on the field for safe playing. When two teams move from opposite directions, remind the players to communicate and be aware of players moving towards them. The type of ball is important here. Be sure to use a nonthreatening beachball and not a heavy ball like a volleyball. Start with a large beachball or try the game inside with a balloon.

Processing: Talk about how the group can communicate during play. You might want to provide paper and pencil for the players to develop a written strategy. Have the players discuss the value of the game as a means of enjoyment, shared responsibilities, and strategy.

Name Game

From Tom Andrews, M.Ed., 1984, who helped us build our first ropes course.

☑ Benefits: The Name Game is a good introductory activity that helps group members learn one another's names, thus enhancing communication among members. One is much more likely to initiate conversation or to communicate thoughts or messages when one knows the person's name.

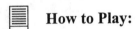 **Equipment:** Two or three soft balls or stuffed animals.

▢ Playing Area: This activity can be played indoors or outdoors in an area large enough for the participants to pass the object back across the circle; i.e., for 12 players a 12 to 15 foot circle offers plenty of room.

Players: Generally best suited for groups of 20 or fewer.

Game Objectives: The activity is easiest to initiate immediately after the group introduction. I prefer to talk to my groups from within the circle. The lead-in to the Name Game may be to express the importance of being able to call out someone's name during an activity or a challenge. How many times are we hesitant to deliver a message because we don't want to say, "Hey, you!" or "You with the red shirt!"

How to Play: To help the participants learn the names, I pick up a ball, say my name, and pass the ball to the person on my right. He or she does the same until the ball gets around the entire circle. After the ball has gone completely around the circle once, the person with the ball calls out someone's name and passes the ball to that person. The recipient then does the same, calling out the name of someone else and passing the ball to that person. After a period of time (maybe two minutes), another ball, even two, may be introduced into the game to keep up the interest. Make sure that the participants call out the names before they toss the ball. During the activity, the group leader will ask if anyone thinks they know all the names. We commonly offer an incentive, generally a frappe, to the first person who gets all the names correct. Not everyone will get all the names correct. Generally, the game is concluded after three or four participants get the names correct, thus meeting the objective of the game.

Safety Issues: Use soft balls that are easy to catch and won't hurt if one is hit in the head. Other objects, like stuffed animals, are often used. Make sure the area is clear of objects that one could trip over as they are going for the catch.

Processing: Ask if they feel freer to talk or call out to another member of the group after learning their name? Help the group recognize the value of learning names both in and out of the group. Ask how many have difficulty remembering names and is it OK when someone asks your name even after you have met them? How does this apply to everyday life? **Note:** Give the game a chance to work, but end it before the interest wanes. Generally five to eight minutes is appropriate.

Nitro Crossing

History takes the origin of this activity back to Hurricane Island, Outward Bound, in 1967.

Benefits: The Nitro Crossing is an activity that lends itself to both individual and group challenges. The activity is good at helping groups to discover the value of community before acting too quickly. The Nitro Crossing is effective in enhancing communication skills, problem solving and team-building.

Equipment: A 12- to 30-foot rope suspended from a strong tree limb or beam. A bucket with either water or six small sticks, and markers (cones, logs, boards, ropes, etc.) to mark the edge of both sides of the ravine.

Playing Area: Preferably outside, but we have often used ropes hanging in a gym or barn. The area should be commensurate with the length of the rope and potential swing but usually for a group of 12 a 15-foot rope, a 20 by 30 foot space offers plenty of room.

Players: Six to 14 participants are ideal.

Game Objectives: The group has a ravine to cross, and the only way to cross it is by using the hanging rope. To enhance the challenge a bit, we tell the group that a hungry pack of 100 mutant wolves are in hot pursuit and will be there in say, 14 minutes. The group receives a small bucket or can containing water or six sticks, six to eight inches long. The water or sticks are the nitroglycerin. (We use the water instead of sticks now for safety.) The group must first get the rope without the use of sticks or any other foreign object but what they have on them. They need to find the best way to get as many as possible of the group or the whole group across the ravine. The nitro is to be used to blow up the ravine after the group gets across. Should one nitro stick be dropped, the whole group will blow up.

How to Play: The rope will hang in the middle of the ravine, which may be designated by two logs, tape, mats, etc. If someone steps over the boundary or touches down when they try to swing over on the rope, they must wait off to the side which is affectionately called "Death Valley."

Modifications: The facilitators can adjust the call on a light touch of the foot to be a "partial loss of that limb," which means the person can use only one foot after that. The distance between the two cliffs is determined by the capability of the group. The group may **not** use sticks to retrieve the rope.

Safety Issues: Spotting is the key in this activity. The most important place for spotters to be is at the landing, where the participants' legs may be over the log and/or group members are tugging one another's legs. Sometimes, arms cannot hold the weight and the participant falls to the ground. Spotters are there to help break that potential fall. Use short nonpointed sticks or water as nitro in order to protect any participants from being hurt.

Processing: Generally the processing focuses upon the need to listen to others (generally in regard to the procurement of the rope) and to believe in your ability as an individual and as a group to succeed.

"Spotting" the Nitro Crossing

140

Ring Game/Object Retrieval

The origin of this activity is credited to Project Adventure.

☑	**Benefits:**	This activity emphasizes communication, both verbal and nonverbal, as well as listening skills.
⁄	**Equipment:**	Basically, all that is needed is a stand secure enough to hold a wooden dowel that is approximately two and a half feet high and a metal ring that is approximately four to five inches in diameter. Attach six to eight strings, each about 10 feet long, to the metal ring. Blindfolds are also needed.
▢	**Playing Area:**	This game is best played in a relatively level field area of at least 30 by 60 yards.
👥	**Players:**	This activity is best for groups of seven to 15 participants. Participants are separated into two groups. The first group is designated as the "nonseeing" group. The second group is designated as the "speaking" group. The "speaking" and "nonseeing" groups should be equal in number. When there is an odd number of participants, one member is asked to volunteer to be the director. With an even number of participants, two members are asked to be the directors.
▦	**Game Objectives:**	To help your blindfolded teammates get the ring over the dowel at the other end of the field without touching your teammates or the rope and using only one-word commands. The objective is for the "speaking" participants to direct the "nonseeing" participants in how to pick up their string. Once all strings are picked up, the group must walk down the field and place the ring over the wooden dowel — using only the strings.
▤	**How to Play:**	Place the dowel stand at one end of a long field. Place the ring, with strings attached, at the other end of the field, from 30 to 80 yards apart. It is important to separate and stretch out the strings to help the participants. The two groups of participants are separated from each other. The "nonseeing" group is taken aside and blindfolded. Each person in this group is paired up with a "speaking" member who will help them through the ac-

tivity. The "nonseeing" group does not know the details of the challenge. The "speaking" participants can only speak to the "nonseeing" participants using one-word action words. For example, "down," "up," "forward," "right," "left," etc. The "speakers" are not allowed to use their hands. They must not touch their partner or the string. The directors, who are not allowed to talk, must help the "speaking" people work together in achieving their goal. As the director points and motions, the "speakers" must communicate through one-word directions to the "nonseeing" people.

 Safety Issues: Make sure the play area is free of holes the players could fall into or objects they could fall over.

 Processing: Communication, frustration, trust.

Ring Game

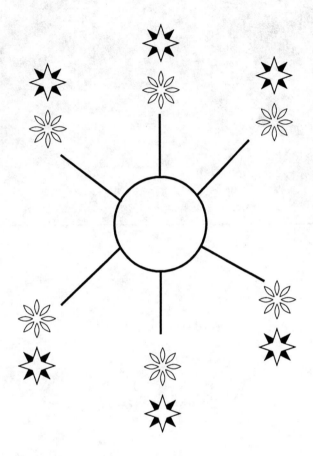

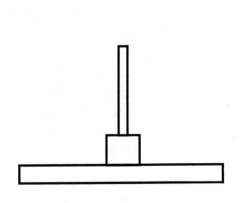

Place the dowel stand and ring, with strings attached, about 40 yards or so apart.

☆☆ Seeing member

❊ Non-seeing member

✾ Director

Ring Game

Shark Bait

This game was an impulsive brain spark at a moment when we needed to create a high-energy team challenge. (*Adventurelore* 1993.)

Benefits: Shark Bait helps develop teamwork and cooperation skills. Equally important is high energy and lots of fun.

Equipment: Several Hoola Hoops are used for the islands, soft balls, or bandannas are used for flags or jewels.

Playing Area: For this activity, you will need a small field or enough space in a large indoor room to accommodate the group. Place a rope at either end of the field to act as end lines. Rope off a small box near one starting line to act as a "jail." At the opposite end of the field, beyond the end line, place 25 to 100 "jewels" (depending on group size.) Hoola Hoops, or any type of large round rings are scattered throughout the length of the field. These serve as safety islands for the "swimmers." The number of safety islands depends upon the size of the group and the length of the field.

Players: Shark Bait is great for groups of eight to 50. Originally designed for small children, it has become a favorite of all ages.

Game Objectives: The group leader explains that the objective of the game is for the whole team to get as many "jewels" as possible to the end line before the time is up (usually 12 to 15 minutes) without being attacked by a "shark." Participants are the shark bait. "Sharks" are staff members who are "swimming" about the field searching for their bait.

How to Play: Participants trying to capture a jewel are able to avoid the vicious shark's attack by standing inside a Hoola Hoop island. One foot in the hoop is safe. Participants who become shark bait must go to jail. Participants are able to get out of jail when another group member delivers a "jewel" to free them. Participants are instructed to only retrieve one "jewel" at a time. The group members must periodically decide whether it is more helpful to the group's goal to release a participant from jail or to deliver the "jewel" safely across the end line. Participants are asked to stand in a single-file line when in jail. "Jewels" will be brought to the first member in the line, so as not to create hard feelings or favoritism among the members.

Modifications: When using this game with younger children, more islands may be added. For an extra challenge with more athletic groups, fewer islands are used. To extend the game, put the "jewels" that are left in the jail by players that are freed back to the end. (This is done by a staff member.)

Processing: Talk about what worked and didn't work for the group. Did the group discuss possible strategies and consequences? How did the participants feel when their team chose to deliver the jewels to the end line, rather than buy their freedom from jail? How did the participants feel about those who helped free them by delivering the jewels to the jail? Discuss risk taking for the good of the group. Was the risk you took well calculated, however spontaneous, or an impulsive action without regard to the outcome?

Shark Bait

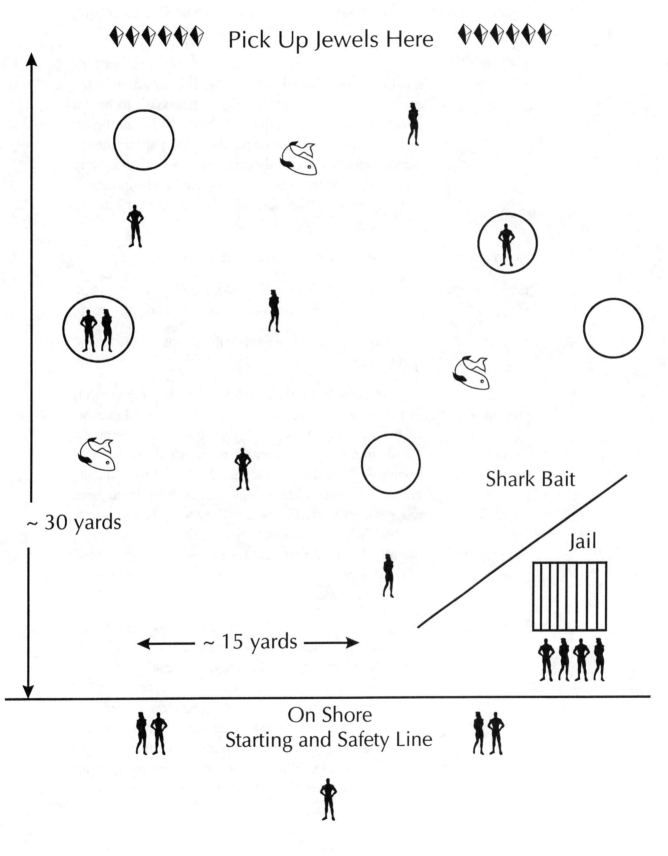

Pick Up Jewels Here

~ 30 yards

Shark Bait

Jail

~ 15 yards

On Shore
Starting and Safety Line

Shipwreck/Titanic II

Turning impulsivity into creativity at a moment when we needed something new, *Adventurelore*, 1997.

☑	**Benefits:**	Shipwreck, most recently titled, Titanic II, is an outstanding opener for any size group. It brings to light the components, means, and attributes necessary to help a group be successful, especially under difficult times. Titanic II provides the opportunity for participants to become more aware of their ability to work as a group for the good of the whole, to be caring and supportive, and to share and be able to communicate effectively with one another.
	Equipment:	A one-foot square board for each participant.
	Playing Area:	For this activity, you will need a small field or enough space in a large indoor room to accommodate the group.
	Players:	This activity can be played with groups of 10 to 500 participants.
	Game Objectives:	After three to five rafts have been removed, the group is instructed to remove 50 percent of the original number of boards, (e.g., they must get 40 participants on 20 boards in a certain amount of time, usually eight to 12 minutes.) They may select their method of reducing boards, or rafts if you will. Those who have been dragged down into the dark will try to work together to get back with the group and to consolidate boards (rafts) as well. The goal is to remove half of the boards; however, groups may be encouraged to try to reduce the number even more.
	How to Play:	Each person is given a one-foot square board on which to stand. The group forms a large circle. The facilitator asks, "How many saw the movie Titanic? What happened in the movie? Why did so many die?" "Not enough life boats," will be the common reply."Yes, that's correct." Do we ever find ourselves without the desired amount of resources (perhaps another example for kids groups)? What do we do when supplies are low? Do we hoard? What happens when greed takes

148

over, at work, with our friends, with family members? Was more room still available on some of the Titanic's lifeboats? Could more people have been saved if everyone had been willing to care and to share? What would you do if a comrade needs help? Let's assume each and everyone of us has our own lifeboat. Shhh . . . There seems to be a leak in one of your boats, and you can't touch the water (referring to the ground underneath) for it is shark infested. And the shark will drag you off into sharkland (approximately 20 yards away). Without touching the water (ground), you must find a way to get back to the group or be forever lost.

Safety Issues: Spotting may be necessary if the participants try to lift or carry teammates on their shoulders. If the activity is done indoors on hard floors, be aware of the boards sliding. Rubber backing to the boards helps prevent this.

Processing: Talk about supportive friends and teammates, ingenuity, communication, trust, teamwork, and the application of the lessons of the exercise to the real world.

Shipwreck

149

Swamp Log Walk

This activity was created by the need to move some leftover logs, which were the result of building our new ropes course. The element adds to the challenge and the excitement of real-life experiences, *Adventurelore* 1996.

☑ Benefits: To help develop self-confidence, healthy risk-taking (there is room for debate here), teamwork, and support for one another.

✎ Equipment: For this activity you will need logs (approximately 10 to 18 feet long), a retired climbing rope, and a styrofoam flotation device.

⬚ Playing Area: To construct this activity, you may want to begin in the winter, when there is ice on the pond or the water source that you wish to use. (We actually use a swamp with live snakes and turtles perched on the log). Place a series of logs, 8 to 16 inches in diameter each, similarly to those shown in the figure on page 154. Join the logs together with a retired climbing rope and place a styrofoam flotation device on the sides of the logs to keep them afloat. As the ice begins to melt, adapt the styrofoam flotation device as needed. And you're ready to go.

👥 Players: This activity works well for groups of two to 30.

▦ Game Objectives: Each group's mission is to get the whole team across the logs without falling in the water) to the other side. The challenge in this activity is two-fold. As you can imagine, wet logs become quite slippery. Team members must help and support each other as they move across the logs, keep one another from falling in, and help someone back onto the log after they tumbled into the "alligator-infested" waters below. The groups must also pass each other on the logs in order to reach the other side, which is an added challenge.

▤ How to Play: This activity is great on a warm sunny day and works well for groups of two to 30. The motivation to complete the challenge successfully might be greater on a colder day. To begin, divide the group in half. One group starts on each end of the log walk. Each group's mission is to get the whole team across the logs (without falling in the water) to the other side.

Modifications: A similar activity is often done on logs that are placed on the ground or sometimes on a wire. The dry ground method can be used as a lead up to the "real deal." However, when these logs are placed in the water, the activity poses real-life consequences for mistakes. When participants realize the repercussions of taking on the challenge alone, or not working together to support and help one another, they are much more likely to conform to cooperative behaviors and begin to use teamwork. Likewise, the repercussions of bailing out on another who may be falling are greater. This, of course, leads to some pretty powerful processing. A change of clothing is recommended for participants in this activity. Flotation may only be necessary on every other log. Try it out.

Safety Issues: Because the logs are in the water, caution must be used as they become wet and slippery.

Processing: Issues around giving and receiving support from group members, addressing fears, and reaching the realization that our perceptions and fears can be overcome by addressing them, are a few of the issues to be addressed in the processing.

Swamp Log Walk

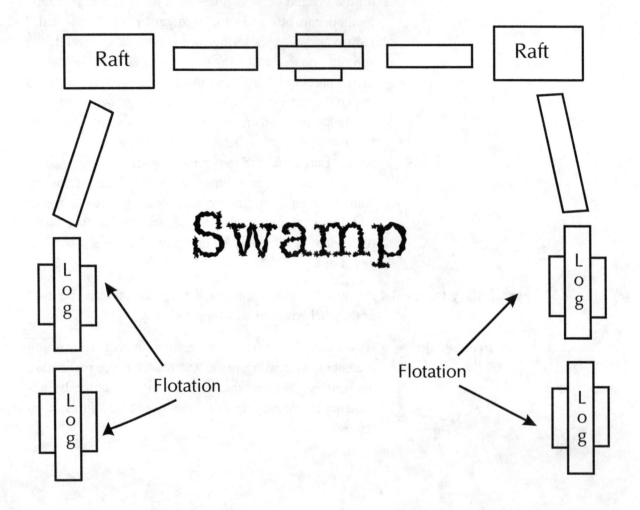

Whoops!

The Tire Tree

Also called King's Finger, by Karl Rohnke while instructing at the North Carolina Outward Bound School.

Benefits: To improve the group-thought process, communication and teamwork.

Equipment: A tire, a 12-foot tall tree stump, some sawdust.

Players: Any size group. If working with large numbers, have several teams.

Game Objectives: The objective is to get a tire over the top of a 12-foot tall tree stump.

How to Play: The Tire Tree is an activity that requires a group effort, both physically and cognitively. This is one activity in which the more physically capable a group is, the less it will have to rely on cognition. The challenge often uncovers the unsung heroes, the pillar masters. The stump should have no stubs or branches sticking out of the sides. We recommend the use of sawdust around the base of the stump. Two or four competent spotters also are recommended for this activity.

Modifications: Staff may assist as pillars, but must not leave the group without a spotter. Sticks may be used if the staff sees that raising the tire is too difficult without them.

Safety Issues: Spotting is essential for groups as they climb. Spotters should be positioned to slow or stop a fall. Make sure the supporting participants are free of physical problems that could injure them as a result of lifting or falling. Staff needs to help the group be acutely aware of a potential fall of the tire and help it come down safely.

Processing: Talk about teamwork, safety, communications, and individual strengths.

Support, struggle, perseverance

11
Summer Adventure Programs

Summer adventure programs are designed to improve the self-confidence, self-esteem, social skills, and perseverance of the participants in a fun and challenging way. "A group living situation in a wilderness setting provides opportunities in which an individual can excel in a variety of areas: cooperating, overcoming fear, organizing, showing compassion, demonstrating responsibility, following directions, solving problems, demonstrating leadership, as well as showing physical ability" (Kolb 1988). Participants range from seven to 18 years of age and may have a school coding, a DSM IV diagnosis, or they may be model students. The conditions for acceptance into the program are that the children must be nonviolent and be physically capable of participating in the various activities offered in that program. Groups are divided into chronological age program placements of seven to 11, eight to 12, 13 to 17, and 14 to 18. The average-size group is 12; however, in many groups eight is an optimal number. The staff ratio is between one to two and one to three. One to four or five is acceptable for many programs.

Adventure-Based Staffing — The Critical Factor

The *Adventurelore* staff consists of about 50 percent professional counselors/psychotherapists, 30 percent teachers, and 20 percent college students majoring in a human-relations field. Most importantly, the staff is carefully selected for their intuitiveness, sensitivity, patience, energy, up-beatness, ability to initiate fun, responsibility, being a strong team member, durability, and willingness to learn and share with other staff. Staff selection is the most important developmental part of the program. Strong counseling and interpersonal skills are the key to effectively working and playing with these children.

The hard skills, such as ropes course competency, canoeing, sailing, orienteering, and others, can be learned and/or improved during the pre-season. A three- or four-day staffing, followed by several days of practical work, help to develop the team. The nucleus of the staff averages eight to 10 years with the program, which adds the value of experience and the knowledge of what to do when.

Perseverance is a key quality for each staff member to have. Not only does a high degree of perseverance make the program run effectively and smoothly under various circumstances, but it models a characteristic that is so important for our youth to learn.

Outward Bound, a front runner in adventure-based programming, originated from the need to teach sailors how to persevere at sea. Outward Bound, as does *Adventurelore* and other similar programs, uses the challenges of adventure-based programming to help people, young and old, transfer their adventure-based survival skills to their nonadventure-based world.

Making difficult challenges fun and exciting helps people to develop a healthier and more effective attitude towards dealing with the difficulties in their lives. Staff must model healthy perseverance and be able to process the children's challenges, attempts, failures, and successes. They need to reach out to children, comfort them, and help them grow from their mistakes or shortcomings. Each time a youth falls short of his or her goal, the staff needs to assist them in making the experience one of growth. As Thomas Edison once remarked, "I didn't keep doing it wrong. I just found a thousand different ways of how to not do it."

Summer Adventure Programs: *"Adventurelore* Style"

The groups generally meet at *Adventurelore* Long Pond at 9:00 a.m. of Day One. Prior to that, the staff should be familiar with each child and the child's needs. In order to facilitate this, we ask the parents for a comprehensive write-up about their child. Each parent is asked to note any special needs, strengths, issues, medications, likes or desires. A picture of each Adventurer helps staff members to make the connection more quickly. Children with special needs are discussed, and a staff member is usually assigned to be that child's primary confidant, unbeknownst to the child initially.

As the Adventurers (we will refer to the clients/campers as Adventurers in the summer program) arrive at the check-in point, staff are there to greet them, make them feel comfortable, and get them involved in an activity. We often use the trampoline, which is fun, nonthreatening, and success oriented. Others may gravitate to the slam-dunk basketball hoop, with staff there to interact and pump them up for the slamming challenge, which is designed to give everyone a taste of success. Once all the Adventurers have arrived, the group forms a circle to discuss the upcoming trip. Usually by that time, a couple of veteran Adventurers have started a week-long wrestling challenge with a staff member, which lightens the mood and makes it clear that we are not a hands-off organization. Equally clear is that we have unequivocal respect for each other. A comfortable, upbeat, humorous welcome is given and the itinerary and rules of the program are reviewed. We have three rules, which, stated generally , are:

Rule #1 — Safety

This will be stated briefly and discussed, reviewed, and re-emphasized as necessary throughout the trip.

- Swim only when staff are present.
- Always wear a life jacket while in water craft; unless otherwise instructed.
- Go no more than four feet off the ground without being on a staff member's belay.
- Camping knives need to be checked in with a staff member.

Rule #2 — No Fighting and No Ridiculing (We need to deal with reality here)
- No physical contact with anyone who you are mad at.
- Respect the feelings of others

When we, as staff, see you as a group being responsible for the physical and emotional safety of one another, then you earn the right to make the majority of decisions as to our daily activities, including when and what we eat, where we stay (within the guided realm of wellness and safety). This has been extremely effective for our adolescent groups.

Rule #3 — Have Fun

After going over the rules, we typically move on to an activity, such as the "Name Game." The Name Game allows the participants to become familiar and less hesitant to communicate with one another. Commonly, we'll then move to an activity that breaks down defenses and physical barriers, and provides an opportunity for team success. Establishing positive teaming at the beginning is important. Challenge games, such as the Human Knot, All Aboard, Hoop Pass, Low Ropes Course, and Lap Sit allow everyone to be fully involved. Trust Leans and Trust Falls helps to establish the awareness of the need to be able to count on the group. At this time, different group approaches are used. The approach, because it depends upon the nature of the group and sometimes upon the weather, is not predetermined. Spontaneity is best! Three general options for our particular program include:

Option One. Continue the group initiatives to develop greater insight on the group and develop a greater cohesiveness. Activities might go in order of Nitro-Crossing, Tire Tree, Acid Swamp, and Board Walk. Process the group activities, then choose the afternoon options of: Ropes Course, Waterfront Activities (Swim Test, Swimming, Canoeing, Sailing, Water-skiing), and/or Capture the Flag. As the day progresses, the group decides whether to experience an overnight at Long Pond or travel approximately two hours to upstate New Hampshire, or more commonly, five hours to Bar Harbor, Maine or to the Franklin Farm (a base camp).

Option Two. Continue with a couple of group initiatives, process, move to the waterfront activities, and head for Maine in time for dinner.

Option Three. Travel to Maine, stop for lunch and activities along the way. Arrive at Franklin Farm in time for swimming, waterfront activities, group games and the first night with the "Wildman" challenge.

The four-and-a-half to five-hour van ride to Maine often sets the social stage for the week. Staff need to be appropriately placed throughout the van. One staff always in the back seat, one in the middle, one towards the front, and the driver. It is very important to set the tone through a proactive trip and to develop the ideal in relating to staff; the ideal being comfortable, open, and respectful rapport among staff and campers. Staff must lead positive conversation, games, and challenges to keep the flow positive and upbeat. Groups vary significantly in regard to the type of activities each group does, as well as the sequence in which they do them. We will, therefore, talk about particular periods of time and individual activities.

Adventurelore's Maine Outpost: The Program

At the farm, the staff talks about safety issues and welcomes the kids to the farm. Safety issues include: use of waterfront activities with a staff member, leaving the premises only with a staff member, using the rope swing with a staff member present, wearing a helmut while mountain biking, having a biking partner and staff approval, and a "don't go near Mrs. McGregor's garden warning." We also stress that matches and knives cannot be used without staff supervision.

After the rules are clearly understood, Adventurers are shown around the premises and establish their bunking arrangements. Then, let the games begin. This is the time during which the group must begin positive development. Without the positive influences, the negative forces will reduce group cohesiveness and foster animosity. Games that include everyone and are active and fun best serve the objectives of the program. Remember, **fun** is the key ingredient in a positive program. Fun also is the mental and emotional lubricant that allows the important lessons of the day to slip into one's awareness.

Capture the Flag is traditionally one of the most popular activities. It combines fun, excitement, challenge, and teamwork. Capture the Flag also gives the staff the opportunity to control the distribution of success so that each person achieves some measure of it, particularly those who need it most but might be at a disadvantage to achieve it. If the competitiveness of the game is too much for the group, we shift to a less competitive, though not less active, game. High-energy games are more popular and reduce anxiety in most of the participants. Because this outing might be the first time some of the Adventurers have been away from home on their own, we want to focus their energies and attention on fun and excitement. Activities such as soccer, Blind Walk, and Tip It work for older Adventurers. For the younger ones, Shark Bait and a rock/paper/scissors type of activity are more appropriate (see Chapter 10). From day one, it is essential to initiate activities that include everyone and to be aware of and to acknowledge individual needs.

Day One

Day One at the farm typically closes with dinner, a time for talking through the events of the day, a "wrestle around," team dodge ball, and a game of "Wildman." Junior groups will generally have a couple of Adventurers who need to be nurtured a little more than others. Although the older groups will have some kids who become homesick, the homesickness shows up in a different way, and the staff still will need to attend to it. These times provide excellent opportunities for the staff to develop or to enhance a caring and trusting relationship. We do, however, caution new counselors to beware of over dependency, which manifests itself usually by day three. As Brobas cautions, "Kids are masters at feigning helplessness when they want to be taken care of, and it is easy for counselors as protectors, leaders, and surrogate parents to fall into that trap. While some campers may genuinely need some of their decisions made for them, such dependency does not lead toward autonomous, problem-solving behavior." (Ewert 1986).

Indeed, a key to that success rests within a staff that is upbeat, friendly, interactive, proactive, clear, concise, and models positive behaviors. Staff needs to stay three steps ahead of the participants, whether in conversation or physical activities, in order to lead the group in positive directions.

Because we work with a high percentage (approximately 35 percent) of Attention Deficit Hyperactive Disordered children, being proactive is essential. Leading these kids in positive discussions and positive activities is so much more effective than punishing them or trying to redirect them. This is true whether we are adventuring, riding in the vans, playing, or sitting at the dinner table. Enthusiasm among the staff gets these kids going.

161

Down time — that period after a day of climbing or canoeing — is typically the most dangerous time for social conflict and homesickness during the summer program. To eliminate or reduce that potential, staff entices the kids into a more positive environment. Typical activities we use are Frisbee, "Tip It," mountain biking, canoe swamps (usually kids against staff), football, soccer, Whiffle Ball, Capture the Flag, volleyball, basketball, Moon Ball, and wrestling. Allowing the kids to participate in small groups of two, three, or four give them time away from the hustle and the bustle of 12 kids. The smaller group also gives the staff the opportunity to give more individual special time.

One Boy's Story — A Case Study

Teddy was a hyperactive nine-year-old boy with a history of failure because he was unable to focus and was highly impulsive. He was the behavioral problem in the classroom, the scapegoat on the playground, and the major cause of turmoil at home.

His pediatrician diagnosed him as ADHD and began a trial of Ritalin. After a few months of medication, subsequent adjustments in dosage and no substantial improvement, Teddy's pediatrician informed his parents that there wasn't anymore that could be done for Teddy and that "they would have to learn to live with him." A few months later, Teddy began counseling at Adventurelore. During his initial visit, we could see the energy radiating from his body and his lack of inhibition. Teddy's history of failure did not subdue him. Leaving Mom's side to scout the area wasn't a problem, either. In a period of ten minutes, we breezed through a dozen different topics as he went from the rope swing, to the trampoline, to kicking a soccer ball around, to the canoes. There was no longer a question about the degree to which Teddy was unable to focus. Teddy, with all his hidden strengths, was truly limited by his impulsivity and inability to focus.

During the few individual sessions prior to the end of school, we worked predominately on success and impulse control. Each session began with some trampoline (mega energy displacement), 10 minutes of talk time to discuss any positives of the week and finished with two activities that Teddy chose. It was crucial for us to reinforce his success in the activities. He loved the activities and grew from his acknowledged success. After session four, we increased the post-activity process time by another 10 minutes. We also focused on transferring his success in the activities to home and school.

After his sixth session, Teddy entered the Adventurelore Summer Program. Although he was quick to make friends, the positive relationships were brief. Teddy's impulsiveness and inability to share and to take turns far overshadowed his endearing qualities. Teddy was setting the stage for social failure and criticism as he had done many times before.

During the evening staff meetings, the "Teddy Saga" took 50 percent of the day's total processing. The concerns strongly supported Teddy's earlier assessment, i.e., that his impulsive behavior was preventing him from establishing any sustained positive social relations. The social rejection continued to reduce his level of self-esteem and his reaction to other children's requests were defensive, which increased the social rejection. Somewhere in the cycle, Teddy needed to experience success and to build upon it.

Our treatment plan was multi-dimensional and included trying to stay ahead of Teddy and maintain a positive mode. We needed to consider many strategies, including keeping him busy with positive involvement, redirecting a potential crisis, providing more one-to-one nonjudgmental time, and allowing for time in which a staff member could accompany Teddy on a walk, a bike ride, or in a canoe to give him a welcomed reprieve from the social stresses. As the stresses built his degree of impulsive behavior and defensiveness heightened. This time was Teddy's time for some positive input on any social or physical success. Occasionally, this private time would include one more child, and it became a special, secret event, or exploration during which we continually rewarded the positive.

Above all, success had to be pumped into the cycle of failure. The success, to be most effective, had to be recognized and, more importantly, appreciated by the group. During a special staff v. kids game of Capture the Flag, we planned to catch most of the kids' teams and put them in jail. The flag was well-guarded, but Teddy "somehow" breaks through and frees the others from jail. Teddy is successful; his team recognizes and appreciates his success.

Through a game of Wildman, (a night game of tag, played without flashlights, in which the kids hunt down staff) Teddy's successes were again reinforced. Anyone who catches a staff member during this challenge activity earns frappes for all. Teddy was the one who caught the staff. He was successful, and his peers appreciated him once again. As one might expect, Teddy was becoming more accepted. He felt better about himself and was less defensive for a variety of reasons. Careful one-to-one special time with a staff member allowed Teddy to gain some insight into his new status and how it could work for him or against him. Teddy agreed to use a cueing system to help him redirect any potential negative interactions with others. Later that week, Teddy retrieved a canoe paddle that another camper had left out in the lake. His energies and improved self-image were working for him. It's not that the four weeks made Teddy a new person or took away his hyperactivity. The experience did, however, give Teddy some success and a break in his cycle of failure. The experience also gave Teddy positive memories, a feeling of self-worth, and some important fuel for his days in school.

During the next year, his teacher was very receptive to ideas on how to help Teddy succeed, and her contribution to his continued success was paramount. If Teddy finished his work early, as he was able to do, he was allowed to use the computer. When Teddy had good days, which were more and more common, he could help the custodian, which of course, allowed Teddy to displace his energy in a positive way. Teddy loved it. The playground, with it's lack of structure and established social pecking order, still was difficult for Teddy, but he did have new friends and showed social growth. As Teddy's therapist, I made weekly contact with home and/or school and rewarded Teddy with extra time and his choice of activities for his good weeks. At home, Teddy began accepting responsibility for a small, well-scheduled job, approximately five to 10 minutes, to help boost his feeling of self-worth at home. The jobs increased in responsibility and so did his self-esteem and his allowance. Three years later (as of this writing), Teddy still enjoyed his bimonthly visits to Adventurelore and his activity time. He would come in, sit down and talk first ("to get it out of the way") before getting into an activity or challenge. Through the efforts of his parents, a sensitive, caring, and cooperative school staff, and sparks of success, Teddy flourished. Three seasons of sports, honors in school, being accepted on the playground, and the responsibility of a major newspaper route had made Teddy an Attention Deficit Hyperactivity Advantaged happy, young man.

Day Two

Day two for junior groups may include an overnight at Donnell's Pond, with canoeing, canoe capsizing, water sports, Island Capture the Flag, and a night hike. The night hike up Scoodic Mountain, after canoeing across the lake in the light of the moon, does wonders to bolster self-confidence and to work on the fear of the dark. In this activity, the hikers must depend upon good communication and trust. Each hiker puts one hand on the back of the hiker in front of him. Where to walk and what to grab for support is communicated from the front of the line. The challenge of hiking in the dark is so exciting that we seldom hear a complaint from anyone about being tired. Hiking can be a vigorous activity, but to hike up a mountain in the dark produces a major boost to one's self-confidence. For the more adventurous of the Adventurers, we offer the option of spending the night on top of the mountain.

Day Three

Day three is spent on water activities, island exploration, a trip to the quarry for optional quarry jumps, another powerful self-confidence booster, as is the two-mile canoe trip back to the vans. The program is designed to have one or more special esteem- and confidence-building challenges a day that are recognized and reinforced by the staff.

Day Four

Day four for the junior groups is typically another mountain hike, with some rock climbing, rappelling, and cave exploration. The early evening may include some sailing and a social visit to Bar Harbor. The night is spent at the Franklin Farm base camp. Wildman is the "number one" nighttime challenge treat. After 17 years of running such programs, we all are a bit amazed when we process the day. After an exciting game of Wildman, we celebrate the successes with frappes, at about 11 p.m., and then we put the Adventurers to bed. In spite of the amount of activity and "frappage," the Adventurers sleep very well.

Day Five

We begin this day with an early wake-up call and end the week's activities with white-water rafting. Once again, these children take on a challenge that might initially seem insurmountable, but they are successful. The successes are reinforced during the campfire program that evening. We emphasize that the staff must stay very sensitive to the mixed emotions the children experience during the final evening. Although it is the last night before the children go home to their families and all the comforts of home, the night also marks the conclusion of one of the most, if not the most, exciting and emotionally powerful weeks of their lives. The last night is a special time to help the children realize the challenges that they have met and to appreciate their achievements and their social, emotional, and physical growth. Careful processing of these milestones emphasizes them in a way that reinforces the strengths that they will carry home, and, eventually, to school.

Games We Play

We do use competitive sports that offer the option for those who enjoy competition to play, to develop sportsmanship, and, for someone who needs it most (staff assisted), to be successful — even be a "hero." Being able to laugh, joke, and wrestle around after a competitive game provides a healthy desensitizing period and the opportunity to purge any residual post-game anxieties that some kids may still carry. It is important to process the feelings of winning and losing in competitive games. Youths who learn to enjoy competitive games, win or lose, are more likely to continue to play as they get older. The heightened self-esteem also will increase the likelihood of good sportsmanship strengthening social relations.

Wrestling is an activity that has become very popular with the *Adventurelore* kids. They love to challenge the staff. In recent years, I have been convinced that adolescents, in particular, have the unconscious need to wrestle their way out of adolescence and into adulthood. Wrestling provides a physical release through physical contact with others and underscores the ultimate responsibility of keeping your opponent (partner) safe. Wrestling teaches the child to respect the safety of his opponent while trying to establish physical control over him. This activity is high on the list of activities that break down physical barriers and develop unconditional respect for others. Points are seldom scored, and the energetic rolling around while staff monitor the smiles and the nonaggressive post-match demeanors are par for the course. A team challenge, initiated by a staff member, to pin another staff member, is common. Of course, a frappe is awarded to each team member after they have completed their goal.

Other methods of establishing self-esteem, which were explained earlier in the individual-therapy section, may be implemented in the group setting as well. Modeling is one of those techniques and deserves additional attention in this section. Things don't always go right during adventure-based trips, and staff are responsible to persevere and to model healthy methods of dealing with failure. In addition to modeling perseverance, staff needs to model self-control and patience. A staff person who loses control, yells at his kids, and is demeaning will not have a positive effect upon his group. When kids see adults out of control, their anxiety becomes heightened. As adults and clinicians, we need to practice what we preach. Stop and think. When the counselor's emotions overrun his cognition and escalated verbiage is the product, he should be quick to apologize. Even this poor, but human, response affords another great opportunity to model.

Adventure-Trip Discipline

Although we can't escape the need to discipline, we should make the discipline as positive as possible. Whenever being proactive can prevent a disciplinary measure, be proactive. When disciplinary actions can result in a consequence that is logically related to the offense, then it can have therapeutic value. Demeaning statements and a loss of temper that are directed at the child are counterproductive.

We have found that giving a sequence of positive reminders can avert disciplinary action. When a child acts out during a discussion or activity, our first means of intervention is direct eye contact. This is followed by a pre-established cue. If that is not effective, we will say the child's name, adding an auditory cue to the earlier visual cue. These measures would typically be followed by a more direct request; sometimes interjecting some humor into the request to help maintain a positive atmosphere. Should the preceding steps be ineffective, an unconditional time-out would likely be used. There are circumstances, however, in which ignoring a behavior is most effective. Depending on the severity of any offense, which could range from disrupting a group to fighting, the length of the time-out will vary. The counselor and the child will talk about the incident before the child is allowed to re-enter the group.

When disruptions occur in a van ride, the same general procedures are applied. If the event is more significant and/or persists, then the child is separated from the group in which the offense took place. From that point, a walk with the counselor is recommended. One-to-one, talk-and-walk therapy for a mile or two helps to bring emotions back in check. This logical consequence gives the child space and restores calm in the van. It also gives the child the opportunity to vent and to get feedback. Although most walks are relatively short, a couple of miles or less, some may require several miles of walking and talking. It's often okay to make light of the consequences, because it teaches the child that an inappropriate action is followed by a logical consequence. A person doesn't need to stay uptight about what happened. Handle the consequence and get on with life. This, of course, does not lessen the importance of the child showing remorse for any harm caused to someone or something. The need for remorse should be thoroughly expressed before going on to something else. Adventurers also need to know how to appropriately handle disciplinary actions at home or school. Teaching the child to persevere and to smile through difficult times does not mean, for instance, that the child should smile at his school principal as he gives the child three detentions for throwing food. Helping the child to make the distinction between the two emphasizes the importance of processing and role playing.

Reducing the intensity of the child's emotional state during a conflict often requires that the child be removed from that situation. If the escalated emotions are within control, the counselor might defuse the intensity with some humor. The counselor might shift or share the focus of attention to alter the direction of the conflict and to avoid confrontation from a highly personalized and defensive position. One might liken the counselor's action to stepping, well-armored, in front of a bullet heading for a kid.

Defusing a Fight

Shawn and Geoff, two feisty adolescents, were at opposite ends of the breakfast log (prime adventure-based seating) when Geoff asked Shawn to pass the milk. Shawn replied, "Hold your horses. I'm not done with it!" Geoff responded, "Your mom likes horses, not cows, so pass it down!" Geoff took offense, got up, and headed for Shawn saying, "You want to talk about my mother?" The counselor approached in an upbeat manner, to prevent any physical contact. He portrayed, through body language as well as speech, a relaxed manner, and took the focus. "You know my mama likes horses, and some may say she's a Palomino, purebred she is. I guess that's why I'm such a good looking stud."

The counselor intervened in a positive, nonthreatening, yet silly, manner and turned the circumstance from a negative confrontation into a humorous event. The counselor's modeling helped the boys to see that it's okay to be part of the joke and that conflict need not arise from being overly defensive. Such a circumstance would likely come up in the day's processing. Kids that have lower self-esteem are more defensive and tend to personalize things more. This is particularly so when the low self-esteem is coupled with a reduced level of social cueing.

When the level of escalated emotions reaches a point where it's determined to be best to remove the child or the adolescent from the area of confrontation, use an unconditional time-out. The counselor can diminish the emotions by subtly commenting on an unrelated fact, such as recognizing a bird, noticing a picture, or remembering something that needs to be done. Taking the focus off of the child and the incident can help to alter the emotional climate. The unconditional time-out is implemented when two kids are involved in a conflict and need time to emotionally de-escalate so that they can discuss (when necessary) the incident in a controlled manner.

As the child or the adolescent becomes calmer, the counselor can ease back into conversation about the incident in a nonaccusatory manner. The counselor can help the child to see the whole picture and talk about ways in which he could have altered his behavior and the conflict. Kids need to be held accountable for their behaviors, however, they must first be able to see all the circumstances more clearly (cognition over emotion). The emotional fog must be lifted. The counselor can use distractions, smiles, time-outs, and/or physical activity. When the intensity is diminished, the counselor can help the child gain intelligent insights into positive healthy behavior. I have yet to find that banging a dashboard or steering wheel helped anyone to recharge a dead battery.

Senior Adventure Programs — Ages 13 - 18

The senior programs are varied in activity choices, however, they have the same basic objectives such as enhancing self-confidence, self-esteem, group integration skills, and social sensitivity. The same three basic rules apply: safety first, respect one another/no fighting, and have fun. The senior groups have the opportunity to determine the direction of their group as soon as they can demonstrate the ability to monitor their own behavior, respect safety, and each other. The positive and very interactive relationships between staff and Adventurers are comfortable yet respectful. This helps prevent any alienation between staff and Adventurers. Through conflict, the adolescent will sometimes use disparity to create a devisive and subtle defiance. When this does happen, we acknowledge it and deal with it early on. Early intervention allows us to maintain the essential positive flow within the group. The staff's sensitivity to such behaviors is key to maintaining the positive energy of a healthy group.

In the past couple of years, these groups have amazed us with their ability to carry on without substantial staff intervention after just three days. Adolescents have a chance to achieve some independence and choose a direction for themselves. Both have been well-earned.

The variety of trips we can take include a nine-day mountain-biking expedition from Canada to Bar Harbor, Maine, using logging roads and trails, a sailing and rock-climbing adventure, a white-water canoeing and rock-climbing trip, and a 15-day high-adventure trip that includes a one- or two-day solo on one of the islands on a remote lake — camper's choice.

All adventure trips are designed to clearly show the individual that he or she is competent and capable of succeeding with a certain degree of perseverance. Daily processing of activities and interactions reinforces the positive social and physical successes, which further fuel the development of positive self-esteem and social skills. The bottom line is, as the children recognize their higher level of competence, they have less to be defensive about and gain new confidence that can be used to strengthen their social performance back home.

One might believe that the children would be most comfortable and integrated on the last few days of the trip, however, we have found that these last two days are often the toughest. The anticipation of their separation from the group and becoming reunited with their families triggers emotions that may become volatile. This phenomena holds true for other programs as well. Thompson (1984) of the Higher Horizons Program, points out that the participants "are so anxious about their return to the community and home, they actually require more support and counseling at this time." Kerr and Gass (1987) note that "regression to earlier stages is often evident in therapeutic programs as participants approach the end of the experience." *Adventurelore* has programs that last for several days or weeks that result in a mixture of emotions that typically will be expressed during the last night or on the ride home. Adventurers will reminisce about the week and talk about going home. They may experience joy and sadness at the same time. This mixture of feelings, coupled with their normal fatigue, can create an emotional mix that can be a therapeutically beneficial, freely expressed emotion or be destructive. The adventure-based counselor needs to be intuitive and sensitive to these emotions. We tell Adventurers that they are likely to experience a mixture of feelings during the last night and day and are encouraged to discuss their emotions, issues, or reflections with us.

During the van ride home, the staff needs to be proactive and positive, injecting a touch of humor. It helps if the staff bears the brunt of the humor. This behavior models a positive response to being the subject of a joke (an area with which many children and more adolescents have difficulty). Moreover, it reduces the likelihood that someone less capable of handling such humor will bear the brunt of the joke. Because some Adventurers are particularly vulnerable at this time, it is important to maintain a positive, upbeat climate for the close of the week. Parting memories that are positive will help etch a positive social experience in the minds of the Adventurers.

Jamie and the Lean-to — A Case Study

Jamie had a conflict during barn badminton with another Adventurer about whose turn it was to play. The other child said he wasn't done playing. Jamie hollered, "You just finished your game!" Robbie responded, "No Way! It's two out of three!" The other player agrees with Robbie. Jamie feels the others had ganged up on him. He starts swinging on the rope between the players. A staff member reminds Jamie that he shouldn't be swinging on the rope while others are playing badminton.

The counselor offers Jamie another option. Instead, Jamie grabs the racket from Robbie's hand, and the counselor steps in. Jamie gets upset and loses control. Jamie is asked to take a time-out, but he is adamant that the disturbance isn't his fault and that he shouldn't be the one to have to leave. Jamie, emotionally out of control, must be escorted from the play area. As they go down by Jamie's tent, the staff member notices the unique structure of the lean-to, which Jamie had built the day before. The staff member comments on it. He shifts his focus from Jamie to the lean-to. He admires it and inquisitively inspects it's detail. "Did another staff help you build this?" he asks. "No, I did it myself," Jamie replies. The counselor asked, "Did you weave those

170

fir boughs together yourself?'' Jamie answers, ''I did everything my-self. I built it all!'' The staff continues questioning Jamie about the elaborate structure of his lean-to. ''How did you bend those sticks like that?'' Enthusiastically, Jamie responds, ''It's easy! (the turning point) I'll show you!'' The staff member is amazed at Jamie's skill. ''I've never seen one built just that way before! Have you built these things before?'' ''No, I just figured it out myself.'' ''Jamie, that's excellent! You've done a lot of excellent things this week. Chris said you did great canoeing, and I know you did the night hike! Of course, I nearly had to carry you up, but you did it!'' (light teasing). ''Yea, right! I led you up the mountain!'' Jamie replied. ''Okay, I must have forgotten! I know you had a little difficulty yesterday in the van ride back from the lake and in the battle at the barn, but it's really been a good week for you. Hey, what happened up there anyway? You've been pretty good about no conflicts this week. Are you getting a bit tired do you think?''

Note here that the first two sentences continue to recognize Jamie's positive accomplishments, and the next two sentences let Jamie know that he had some ownership in the conflict, and that Jamie needs to recognize how he could have handled it better. The staff member has demonstrated an unconditional, friendly, and nonthreatening demeanor, even though he feels Jamie did something wrong. Jamie perceives that he doesn't have to defend his actions as much because he is already accepted. His emotions are lessened, and he has received recognition for his success. Now he can talk, still with some bias, of course, about how he can better empower himself to prevent conflict.

A word of caution is necessary here. As counselors, we must always be aware that a child in Jamie's circumstances, one who has received so much positive one-to-one attention after a crisis, might subconsciously create another crisis as his needs arise. Jamie did not, but counselors must stay aware of this possibility. When it does happen, and it will, the counselor should deal with it appropriately and quickly. When in doubt, we prefer to err on the side of the positive to continually strengthen self-esteem. Groups and individuals need to know that we are unconditionally there for them to support their efforts, to help them succeed, and to recognize and to praise their successes, whether they are social, emotional, or physical. To facilitate a positive group, the staff must be intuitive, energetic, sensitive, and able to persevere in difficult and trying times.

Group-Experience Processing

In processing the day's experience in a large group, typically eight to 15 participants on a full day and/or multi-day adventure, we offer these pointers:

- Establish a regular time for processing, such as at the end of the day or at a given time each day, and tell the group when the processing will take place.

- Sit the group in a circle on the ground, the floor, or a mat. This arrangement allows for greater focus and a more effective and open dialogue.

- Keep the opening upbeat and positive, such as "Great job on getting through those last rapids! How many of you got wet?" Such comments recaptures the vividness of the experience, refreshes the thought process, and opens an avenue for conversation. We caution you not to be redundant in methodology or to become predictable. What might work well for one group might be less effective for another one. Trust your intuition. Be sensitive to the verbal and nonverbal cues. Remain flexible.

- Give ample time for the participants to answer the questions. Don't worry about any lull in the conversation, because it may take them a few minutes to process the question, to consider the responses already given and to review their experience. You might even wish to rephrase the questions.

- Use metaphorical, real-life situations to help the participants transfer the skills gained during the adventure.

For example:

- Relate the success a child had while climbing the rock face. Recount how he was searching for hand holds and listening to a supportive belayer who could help him to see potential places to grab. As eager as the child was to be on to the next firm grip, he had to put his full trust in the belayer below. This experience reinforces, in a big way, the need to listen and trust and the value of those skills.

- Relate the experience of the group that had to devise a way to get a group member with special needs over the mountain. Thinking through the problem, coming up with a solution, organizing the materials, and getting the job done so that the special member could go on shows caring for another individual and responsibility.

Take care of physical needs before you process an overnight program. When the Adventurers are tired and hungry, they will focus on those needs. Do the processing with a snack while dinner is being prepared. If the nature of the group makes it impractical to begin the processing in this way, wait until after breakfast the next day.

172

Children who are rested and fed are more ready and capable to handle the processing. (Timing is important. Try not to force the processing. Find an appropriate time and way to bring the group into the processing with vigor.)

Good-Byes and Follow-Up

As we return to home base and unload the gear, we are greeted by a gang of parents who are anxiously awaiting their children. This can be, and often is, a difficult time. The responses range widely, from child to child. For some there will be hugs and expressions of joy and excitement. For others, there will be only a brief "hello," after which the child returns to his new-found friends to exchange addresses and that moment of final good-byes. Staff need to be aware of the potential for awkwardness during this time and help to model positive and strong farewells.

Some Adventurers will try to tell their parents about the entire week in five minutes, others however, are beset with directions from their parents to find this and that thing and a negative "How could you have lost it?" Our observations of this brief time are helpful, because we still must prepare to meet with the parents in a post-program session. Every clue that we can garner will help us to gain insight and to tie the experiences of the Adventurer to changes at home and in school.

We end this time with a slide show for the children and their parents. The presentation, which shows our week in chronological order, accomplishes two important objectives. First, it reinforces the many positive images of the social interaction and the significant achievements. Second, it gives the parents an opportunity to share their child's moments of honor and success.

As we end the week, the staff will process the adventure individually with the parents. Included in this session, whether we are talking about a child who was with us for counseling or one who attended mainly for the adventure, is a recap of the child's significant experiences, an assessment of the child's strengths and weaknesses, and our recommendations for the future. We prepare written reports that are available to the parents who request them and for the school, therapists, and state agencies. We invite all of the above to contact us with their questions. It is important to augment the personal benefits with insights and suggestions for school, family, and/or home therapists.

In September, we send out an evaluation/suggestion sheet that helps us to assess our own strengths and weaknesses. We score exceptionally high in meeting the needs of self-confidence, self-esteem, and teamwork. We need to improve in making sure the kids brush their teeth and do not lose things. We're working on it, but if you're looking for daily showers, you're looking at the wrong program. We provide biodegradable soap and plenty of ponds, rivers, and lakes. Oh, the luxuries of home . . .

12
Conclusion

In the preceding chapters, we have given you a condensation of the *Adventure-lore* program. We know that we enjoy unique resources, resources that are not readily available to all who would develop a program such as this. Although it is helpful to have access to the challenge and adventure-based activities that we do, we cannot emphasize strongly enough that the key to success lies not with mountains, ropes courses, and canoeing. The success of an adventure-based counseling program depends upon the enthusiasm, the sensitivity, the energy, the preparation, and the instincts of the counselor.

More than likely, you, as a counselor, do not have access to many of the elements explained in this book, so we suggest that you take a careful, detailed look at the resources that are available in your particular area and in neighboring areas. For instance, a walk in the woods or in a park, takes the counseling session outside the sterile environment, an environment that often does more to build barriers than it does to help the client. Building models and completing other such projects also can add to the comfort and the self-esteem of the client, as well as to the comradeship and the trust between the counselor and the client. Pets or a garden can be used to improve the growth and the sense of nurturing in the client. Hiking, biking, basketball, skating, orienteering are just some of the activities that can spark that light in the eyes of your client. Just use our suggestions and your imagination to create a therapy program that will touch your client in an energizing and positive way.

Regardless of how you establish your program, the objectives of adventure-based counseling remain the same — to provide activities that heighten the experiential process and bring meaning to life and to establish a more personal relationship between the counselor and the child. Adventure-based counseling offers new tools to help the therapist to develop a trusting and comfortable relationship. Although positive and sincere communication forms the foundation for this kind of relationship, adventure-based counseling opens new avenues for growth through action.

Activity is a powerful tool to help the client recognize the need to change, to plan, and to take action. As the client develops a greater trust with the therapist, he will be more receptive to listening and to expressing his feelings. When the client's self-confidence is enhanced, he becomes more likely to believe that he can make a plan and stick to it. With increased self-esteem and communication skills, the client is better prepared to take that important action. The experienced adventure-based counselor can make the initial assessment, develop the rapport, help the client to design a course of action, and to follow through with the design.

Be very clear in your mind that adventure-based therapy is work. It is far more than entertaining your client for an hour. As a therapist, you must make a positive connection. You must be able to assess and develop a positive therapeutic relationship, provide the tools that will foster the development of healthy self-esteem and improved self-confidence, confront inappropriate behaviors, and help the client set goals and take action on those goals. You will do much of this outside the comfort and the familiarity of your office.

The application of adventure-based therapy requires a methodology. Adventure-based therapy employs creative insights to build the essential foundation on which the client can build a stronger self to take into the real world and be successful. It puts communication and conflict resolution in the forefront of the client's welfare. Then, when the counselor has combined the best of his skills, his personality and character and his desire to help the client, the client learns to take positive action to improve his life. A counselor can open no better door for any client.

References

Bourne, Edmund J. *The Anxiety and Phobia Workbook.* Oakland, Calif.: New Harbinger Publications, 1996.

Erickson, Erik. *Child Development.* Dubuque, Ia.: William C. Brown Co. Publishers, 1978.

Ewert, Alan W. *Outdoor Education Pursuits: Foundations, Models and Theories.* Columbus, Oh.: Pub. Horizons, 1989.

Feeney, Judith. *Adult Attachment.* Sage series on close relationships. Thousand Oaks, Calif.: Sage Publications, 1996.

Fitts, William Howard. *Interpersonal Competence: The Wheel Model.* Research monograph Dede Wallace Center; no. 2. Studies on the Self-Concept and Rehabilitation. Nashville, 1970.

Hallam, Richard S. *Anxiety, Psychological Perspectives on Panic and Agoraphobia.* London; Orlando, Fla.: Academic Press, 1985.

Kolb, David A. *Experiential Learning: Experience as the Source of Learning and Development.* Englewood Cliffs, N.J.: Prentice-Hall, 1984.

Lazarus, Arnold A. *The Practice of Multimodal Therapy: Systematic, Comprehensive, and Effective Psychotherapy.* Johns Hopkins paperbacks ed. Baltimore: Johns Hopkins University Press, 1989.

Schoel, Jim, Paul Radcliffe, and Dick Prouty. *Islands of Healing: A Guide to Adventure-Based Counseling.* Hamilton, Mass.: Project Adventure, 1988.

Wilson, Renate. *Inside Outward Bound.* Charlotte, N.C.: East Woods Press, 1981.

Suggested Readings

Bourne, Edmund J. Ph.D., *The Anxiety and Phobia Workbook*. Oakland, Calif.: New Harbinger Publications, Inc., 1996.

Corey, Gerald et al. *Group Techniques,* Revised ed. Pacific Grove, Calif.: Brooks/Cole Publishing Company, 1987.

Corey, Gerald and Marianne Corey. *Groups: Process and Practice,* 2nd. ed. Pacific Grove, Calif.: Brooks/Cole Publishing Company, 1982.

Minor, Joshua, and Joe Boldt. *Outward Bound, U.S.A.* New York: William Morrow and Company, 1981.

Priest, Simon, and Michael Gass, Ph.D. *Effective Leadership in Adventure Programming*. Champaign, Ill.: Human Kinetics, 1997.

Rohnke, Karl. *Funn Stuff.* Volume I - 1995, Volume II - 1996, Volume III - 1997. , Dubuque, Ia.: Kendall/Hunt Publishing Company.

Rohnke, Karl, and Steve Butler. *Quicksilver*. Project Adventure, 1995.

Rohnke, Karl. *Forget Me Knots,* 2nd ed. Dubuque, Ia.: Kendall/Hunt Publishing Company, 1994.

Schoel, Jim, Paul Radcliffe, and Dick Prouty. *Islands of Healing: A Guide to Adventure-Based Counseling*. Hamilton, Mass.: Project Adventure, 1988.

Sullivan, Ilene. *Physical Educational Games for Classroom Teachers — Let's Move and Learn K-4*. Dubuque, Ia.: Brown and Benchmark, 1996.